Tips
on Having
a Gay (ex) Boyfriend

For Emily and Doug, Betty and Lew,
With love

For Ned
Because he believed and he is missed

Carrie

Jones

Tips
on Having
a Gay (ex) Boyfriend

Woodbury, Minnesota

First Edition
First Printing, 2007

Book design by Steffani Chambers
Cover design by Ellen Dahl
Cover image © 2006 Brand X Pictures
Editing by Rhiannon Ross

Flux, an imprint of Llewellyn Publications

The Cataloging-in-Publication Data for *Tips on Having a Gay (Ex) Boyfriend* is on file at the Library of Congress.
   ISBN-13: 978-0-7387-1050-1
   ISBN-10: 0-7387-1050-4

Flux
A Division of Llewellyn Worldwide, Ltd.
2143 Wooddale Drive, Dept. 0-7387-1050-4
Woodbury, MN 55125-2989, U.S.A.
www.fluxnow.com

Printed in the United States of America

```
E-------3------3---------------3---------|
A--------3-------3-------------3---------|
D-----------0------0---------0-----------|
G-------------0------2----X--------------|
B---------------X-------0---3------------|
E------------------3-------X-------------|
```

Saturday

HE WANTS TO KNOW WHY it happens.

"Why," he asks. "Why?"

You shake your head.

"I don't know," you tell him.

He leans back on your mother's stupid corduroy couch, looks away. With his index finger, he flicks a leaf from her tropical plant. He waits for you to talk.

What are you supposed to say?

WE WALK OUTSIDE FIRST. WE walk outside beneath the October stars and hold hands in the cold, cold air. The dim light from neighbors' windows wishes us well. No cars drive by because there aren't that many people in Eastbrook, Maine, driving around at eleven, a sad fact but true.

I wait and walk, quiet, because in the house Dylan said he had something important to tell me. I figure it has to do with college next year, seeing other people, that whole thing, all that stuff we've already decided about how we'd finish out this year and the summer together and then see how things go. His mouth makes a cute little worried line the way it does right before he has an advanced algebra test. I want to kiss it, make him stop worrying about the things I know he's worried about.

The cold keeps me from reaching up and kissing my lips against that cute line. Every time I open my mouth, the cold shrieks my teeth. We walk past the houses in my little subdivision. It's just a mile of road with homes stacked along the sides. That's what it's like in Eastbrook, subdivisions spaced out on miles of rural roads, blueberry barrens and forests scattered between. Every subdivision is far from one another, but the houses clump together. Everyone here knows everyone's business.

I imagine that Eddie Caron had turned away from his NASCAR reruns and watches us trot down the street. Or maybe Mrs. Darrow has pulled aside her curtain and shut off the light in her living room so that she can peer out and see if we kiss. Tomorrow they'll tell their friends and then by Monday everyone will know that Mrs. Darrow saw us kiss, that Eddie Caron saw us act moony beneath the stars.

That's just how Eastbrook is, everybody knows everybody and most of the time that makes me scream and want to hide in a city somewhere, but tonight it just makes me a little warmer in the cold, makes me feel like if Dylan and I fell down, frozen solid from the cold, someone would come and pick us up, call an ambulance, make things okay.

"It's freezing," I say to Dylan.

"Yeah."

"You think Eddie Caron's watching NASCAR?"

"Probably porn."

I laugh, but Dylan doesn't even smile. I make an attempt at humor. "*Bodylicious Babes in Big Trucks.*"

Dylan doesn't say anything. Normally, he'd come back with something like, *Nasty Housewives and their Vacuum Accessories.*

"Dylan, what's up?" I say. "It's cold out. Want to go back?"

He shakes his head. "Give me a second, Belle. Okay?"

Cranky. Cranky. I pull my body a step away from his. I march around the cracks on the road, made by last winter's frost, pushing up the tar, heaving things around. It's almost winter again and still the town hasn't fixed the road. I hop over the cracks to try to warm up.

In my pocket lumps the note Dylan wrote me in school Friday. I always keep his latest note in my pocket like a good luck charm or maybe proof that I have a boyfriend. In case I face the boyfriend inquisition, I can whip it out and say, "No. No. He exists. Really. Here. Here's a note."

Like everyone in Eastbrook doesn't already know that.

The note in my pocket heavies my hip.

"Belle Philbrick, I love you," he wrote, "and if I seem weird today it's 'cause the dark days are getting to me. I hate when the days get shorter."

Maybe that's what's wrong, I think. Maybe it's because it's getting so cold and so dark out. The wind swirls some dead leaves across the road. I shiver.

Dylan stops walking, runs his free hand through his blonde hair, then turns to face me. He takes my other hand in his, the way men do when they propose. In the dark light, I can't tell that his eyes are green. They are just shadows, sad shadows. I shiver again. I want to go inside.

"Belle," he says, voice serious, voice husky. This voice sounds nothing like his normal voice, all mellow and song-like. A cat screeches down the road and it makes us both jump. I laugh because of it but Dylan doesn't. He just stares and stares and starts again with that same serious voice. He sounds like a dad. "Belle, I want you to know that I'll never love another woman."

Not this again. I groan. Dylan is a skipping CD sometimes, stuck on the same track so I give him my normal response and think about how good it'll feel when all this is over and we can go snuggle on the nice warm couch in my nice warm house. "That's stupid. You'll love lots of other women."

He shakes his head.

"You will!" I say and repeat the lines I've been telling him all fall. "And that's okay. That's what happens in relationships sometimes. Love isn't always an exclusive thing. We'll take a break from each other in college and you'll find girls who are way way prettier, and way smarter and way sexier than—"

He drops my hands and throws his own hand in the air. "Will you shut up for a second?"

"Hey . . ." My blood presses hot against my skin and I almost like it, because it isn't cold.

"I am trying to tell you that I will never love another woman." He accentuates every word. A dog barks. They sound the same.

"And I'm saying you will." I blow on my fingers to keep them from freezing.

"No, I won't! I won't! Alright?" He whips around, walks away two steps, and comes back.

A plane flies above us. Its lights blink. It's on its way to Europe probably. Sometimes when planes leave from Boston or New York they have emergency stops in the little airport nearby. It's the last stop before Europe, the last chance for planes and crews. It's a tiny airport but it's got the longest runway in the nation, just a big strip of asphalt with nowhere to go but up.

Ice cracks on a stream behind me and I jump at the bang, but Dylan's body stays still. His face though, turns hectic. He yanks in a breath. I wait for the explosion that always comes when his lips disappear and his fingers curl into themselves. I am not scared. I know him too well to be scared. He would never hurt me. The plane gets farther away.

Instead of an explosion, his voice is steady and strong, "I won't ever love another woman because I'm gay."

The world stops.

One century passes. Two. My mouth drops open. My legs bring me backwards, one step, another, and into the breakdown lane beside the road. My hand finds my mouth and covers it.

Dylan moves toward me, his hands outstretched. "I'm sorry, Belle. I had to tell you."

My head nods. My mouth stays open but no words come out. My body slumps into itself and I crumble down onto the cold ground at the side of the road. It's a praying position, on my knees, hands in front of me.

Dylan kneels too, and hugs me into him. "I love you, you know."

I don't say anything. What can I say?

- - - - o - - - -

It isn't every day that my high school boyfriend, Eastbrook High School's Harvest King, for God's sakes, tells me he's gay. It's not every day that the Harvest Queen is dumped in the middle of a road in my mother's silly subdivision with the stars watching the humiliation and the dogs barking because they want to come help tear my heart out and leave it on the cold, gray ground.

It isn't every day that my entire world falls apart.

"It's okay," I tell him when I can finally talk again and

the chill from the ground has sunk into my bones and my butt. "It's really okay."

"You're not mad at me?"

"No," I say, because I'm not. Stunned, yeah. Mad, not really. Somehow, mostly numb. I unfold my legs and try to stand, but I am slow, slow, slow from the cold.

"Good," Dylan starts whimpering. He sits down and I stop standing. Caught half up and half down, I wrap my arms around him. The dog barks again. Dylan's body shakes against mine. "Good."

I hug him tighter. He sniffs into my hair. His hands move across my back and I tingle, even though, even with what he just told me, I still tingle.

His tears turn to sobs. "I couldn't handle it if you hated me, Belle. I couldn't handle it."

"I know," I say. "I know. I don't hate you."

My words are dark breath clouds in the cold air. My hands pat his back, his hair. I hold on and hold on because I'm scared I'll never hug him again. I hold on and hold on but my heart is empty like the night sky. The plane is gone. It's flown away. Even the dog is quiet.

"We're always supposed to be in love," he says. "We're always supposed to be there for each other."

"Yeah," I say. "We are."

Car headlights swing into the road and I can tell that it's a Chevy pickup truck, which is pathetic, but that's what it's like in a small Maine town. I even can tell by the hitch in the engine that it's Eddie Caron, so I guess that's even more pathetic, but I'm glad he wasn't stuck home watching porn on a Saturday night.

He stops the truck near us and opens the door, but doesn't get out, just sticks his head and part of his body out. It's all black shadow and I can't make out the features that go with his bulk because the headlights are so bright.

"You guys okay?" he yells.

"Yeah," I yell back, which is a total lie.

"You aren't getting funky on the side of the road are you?"

I stand up. "No! Jesus, Eddie."

He laughs. "Just wanted to make sure you're okay, Belle."

"Thanks," I yell back.

Eddie shuts the door and drives to his house. I reach down to Dylan and help him up off the ground.

"We have to get inside," I say. "It's too cold out here."

Dylan doesn't use my hand. He pushes himself up, wipes dead leaf crumbs off his butt. "I hate Eddie Caron."

"It was nice. He just wanted to make sure we're okay," I say.

"Well, we're not. We're not okay, are we?"

He starts walking to my house, not waiting for my answer. It's an answer that would have to be, totally be, a no.

----o----

It's the chorus in a song that he says over and over again. He wants to know why it happens. Why, he asks. Why?

I shake my head.

"I don't know," I tell him.

He leans back on my mother's stupid corduroy couch,

looks away. With his index finger, he flicks a leaf from her tropical plant. He waits for me to talk.

What am I supposed to say?

I can't. I can't say anything.

- - - - o - - - -

We sit on the couch for hours. My mom pokes her head in. She's wearing her turquoise bathrobe, with the little pink roses on it. Dylan is the only person other than me who has seen her in it. She pads over to the couch, yawning. "I've got to hit the sack," she says.

She kisses me on the top of my head, then she kisses Dylan. She squints her eyes at both of us like she maybe knows that something's going on.

"Don't stay up too late, you two," she says and waddles out of the room, heading up the stairs.

"Your mom is so cute," Dylan says, leaning forward. He puts his head in his hands. His voice cracks. "I'm going to miss your mom."

I reach out my hand and touch him on the back. "We'll still be friends. You'll still see my mom."

He shrugs, but doesn't take his face out of his hands. I am stuck staring at the muscles of his back. "It's won't be the same."

"No," I say, wanting to take my hand away but too afraid that it would be insulting somehow, if I moved it. "No, it won't."

We sit like that for a long time. Minutes click away and still I am numb. With each second that passes, Dylan-and-

Belle becomes a lost fairy tale, an old story, and I don't know where this new story is going.

Finally, Dylan sits up. His green eyes look like leaves blending all together. "We'll still sing together, right?" he asks me. "You'll still play Gabriel and we'll hang out. Right?"

I nod, but I know it isn't probably true so I say, "I don't know, Dylan. I don't know. It's like the songs we had, they're gone now. You know?"

He closes his eyes because this is the hardest truth of all.

- - - - o - - - -

Dylan and I would come home after all our extracurriculars were done at school, and we'd always hang out in my bedroom. I'd strum Gabriel and we'd fool around, singing songs, making up chord progressions, fooling around with corny lyrics. Then we'd throw on some old-time crooner music that Dylan liked and we'd sing it.

The thing about my guitar, Gabriel, is that she's how I express myself. I'm not a brilliant writer, or an actress, and I don't spew out heartrending confessional poems. I just play my guitar and that's where all my emotions go.

I bring her to school every day, play her during the second part of lunch, because that's how you get good, you do things all the time, you keep on playing and working at it. I thought that was how relationships were too, but obviously I thought wrong. I didn't factor in the whole gay thing.

I'm not wrong about what playing Gabriel means though.

And when I played for Dylan, all those songs were

about fun and silliness and love and that's gone now. It's all gone.

----o----

Hours later, my mom snores in her bedroom. The clock tells me it's too late to call Emily, my other best friend. Dylan? Well, I can't exactly call him. He kissed me on the cheek before he drove off. My lips felt neglected, but they didn't pout. They trembled instead.

I pull his last note out of my pocket, read another line.

I wish that people would just leave us alone. Leave everyone alone so they can all be themselves. But, of course, there's always a restraint on like a leash.

I read another line.

I just want to be free with you.

Standing in my bedroom, with my flannel pajamas on, it hits me: I will always be lonely.

This stupid note isn't going to help me. I throw it on my dresser and it flutters down on top of my lip gloss, dead.

The stupid clock keeps making it later, too late to call anyone, or even text message.

Gabriel leans up against the wall by the window. She belonged to my dad. I named her Gabriel, which is a man's name, I know, but she's still a girl guitar. She's too pretty to be a boy, and Gabriel was an angel, right? And to me, angels are sort of sexless; they aren't about gender, they're just about soaring and flight, like music. So no matter how much Dylan used to tease me about it, I think it's a perfectly appropriate name for a guitar. I'd play her and Dylan would sing with me, old folk songs mostly. Bob Dylan. Greg Brown. John Gorka. I pick her up, but even arching my fingers over a simple G7-chord doesn't feel right, so I put her back down.

There's a big empty hole in the middle of an acoustic guitar. The sound echoes in there, but right now, that circle looks like an eye staring at me, waiting for me to make some noise, to fill up the empty, but I can't. I'm too empty myself.

Usually, when I'm not at school, or doing homework, or eating, I'm playing Gabriel. The tips of my fingers are hard because of all the strumming I do. Dylan used to call me Guitar Girl. Some people at school still do when we're just hanging out and fooling around. What are people at school going to think? About me and about Dylan?

I touch Gabriel's neck with one of those hardened fingertips, but I can't pick her up. I can't play her.

I turn off my bedroom lamp. Through the window, past the mostly leafless trees and a good mile away on flat land, cars move on the Bayside Road. Their headlights make little lights, like tiny stars. I probably know everyone in those cars and they probably know me. It's probably Dr. Mahoney going in to Maine Coast Memorial Hospital to deliver a baby. It's probably Cindy Cote, Mimi Cote's mother, going in to work her shift at Denny's, our town's only restaurant that serves after 8:30. She works there and at the Riverside on Sundays.

And all those people know me too. *That's Little Belle Philbrick*, they'll say, *whose dad died in the first Gulf War when she was a baby. She dates that cute Dylan boy. What a good couple they are. They'll get married after college. You just can tell.*

In my town, everyone repeats your past and predicts your future every single time they see you, even though the people they tell it to already know. I wonder what they'll say about me now, what they'll say about Dylan.

I turn away from my window and tiptoe through the house without flicking on any lights. It doesn't take much to lose my way, even though I've lived here all my life. Everything is different in the dark. I bump into the coffee table. My shin bruises. My hip launches into the corner of the kitchen counter. The pain is sweet, like water after a long bike ride uphill.

Night sounds skim against me. My mother's snore-breaths bound down the hall. Cars on faraway roads rev their engines. Mice rustle in the walls. Cats' paws pad along crackling leaves.

I lean against the counter.

"I'm lonely," I say to the sounds, the house, to nothing.

In the dark, dark kitchen my body slumps onto the counter, leaning, but my soul, it floats up by the ceiling, watching it all, wondering about this lonely girl with her feet planted on the wood floor, this girl who is me.

My mother snores in her bedroom. The clock tells me it's too late to call.

```
E--------3-----3------------------3---------|
A--------3-------3--------------3---------|
D-------------0------0------------0-----------|
      Sunday
G---------------0------2----X------------|
B----------------X-------0----3---------|
E-------------------3-------X---------|
```

IN THE MORNING, AFTER THE gloom of a typical overcast day wakes up my mom, I leave the kitchen, where I've moved from the floor to the top of the counter.

"Good morning, sweetie. You're up early," she says in her sleep-heavy voice. She makes her way to the coffee-maker, eyes barely open and not really registering anything. She is not a morning person.

"Yep," I say.

I go in my room, ignore Gabriel, and turn on the stereo. It's Barbra Streisand, this super-crooner lady that Dylan loves. She's got this CD of show tunes that came out way back in the 1980s some time. Dylan and I sing to it together. He's a great singer, with one of those musi-cal-classical choir voices. He's an all-state, all–New England baritone. I'm an alto and I'm more folk. When I sing you expect to hear a guitar with me.

But I don't turn on my music. I turn on his. This is ironic, of course, because he's just dumped me, and here I am in my room listening to his music. I can't help it. I turn it up louder and remember.

Sometimes Dylan would sing to me. Sometimes he would sing even if I didn't ask him to, like when I was nervous or we thought I might have a seizure. I'd rest my head on his stomach and his breathing would change, it would become deeper and longer. The breaths flowed out music words that would soar around the room or outside and then flit gracefully into my ears. Even when he sang in chorus, I could always pick out his voice. It was the voice that cascaded into my head, down through my throat, and settled into the depths of me.

I put up the volume real loud because my mom's gone out to the grocery store.

Barbra's got this voice that goes loud and soft and spirals all over the place. I pluck up Muffin, scratch her kitty head, and stare out the window while Barbra sings.

Muffin puts her paw on the cold pane of glass. I close my eyes and hear Dylan's voice mixing with Barbra's.

We'd always come to my house after school and sing this with my stereo. We'd belt out old show tunes, the stuff Dylan really liked. We'd get overdramatic and laugh so hard we couldn't sing anymore. We'd flop on my bed and start kissing. That was our routine.

Dylan can sing everything—folk songs, opera, show tunes, rock. Although, he's not too good at rock. No offense to him. It's too brash for our music breathing. It's not Dylan.

Although, how can I know that? How can I know who he is anymore? And if I don't know who he is, how can I know who anyone is?

I open my mouth and try to sing but just a gulp comes out, like I'm gasping for air. Muffin puts her paw on my face, I breathe her in . . . cat fur, and outside smells like the forest. She purrs.

"Muffin," I whisper to her but I'm not sure if my voice makes it into the outside air or can be heard over Barbra. I close my eyes and lean my forehead against the window, remembering things that are not healthy to be remembering when it turns out that your boyfriend is gay. I do it anyways.

One time after Dylan and I sang this song, we made love and then took a bath. We folded our bodies into the tub and put in raspberry bubble stuff. We laughed and laughed and made bubble beards and bubble boobs and bubble hair and then the bubbles started popping. They just weren't there anymore and the water left the world of hot and journeyed into the world of lukewarm and Dylan kissed me a long, long kiss. Then we just sat there facing each other and everything in the whole bathroom seemed to glow—the tissue box that my mother made with plastic rectangles and yarn, the peach-colored towels, the photo of a southern plantation above the toilet. But mostly it was Dylan. Dylan glowed.

We looked at each other and then this weird, good beam of golden light came out of my eyes and drifted toward Dylan. And at the same time this good, weird beam of golden light shifted out of Dylan's eyes and touched my beam of light. They just stayed there, mingling for a minute. They just stayed there and with them came peace and comfort and all those Hallmarky cheese ball things.

In the water, we sat. In the water, we were silent. In the water, we waited and waited until it was cold. Then we pulled ourselves up and out. The only noise was the water dripping off our bodies and rejoining the water in the tub.

Dylan gave me his hand and we toweled each other off with good rubs.

"I love you, you know," Dylan said, pulling on his jeans. He had to tug them up, because I hadn't dried off his thighs well enough.

"Good," I laughed, reaching around my back to snap my bra. My shoulders stretched. I was still thinking about the light thing, and whether it was just some freak weird hallucination/illusion, or whether it was real. I didn't want to mention it though, because what if he didn't see it? I needed it to be real.

Dylan turned me so my back was against him. His body felt warm. "I'll do that for you."

His fingers snapped my bra closed. He kissed my neck. I shivered. He gently pulled out my ponytail holder and said, "You love me too, right?"

"Yeah." I raked my fingers through my wet hair and turned around to face him.

He tilted his head like a dog does when it's trying to figure something out. "How much do you love me?"

"With all my soul," I said. I believe it too. I believe that's how I love Dylan, even though it's corny. And I believe that afternoon, in my bathtub, we saw our souls. It was the only time in my life anything remotely magical happened. And I was going to keep believing it. No matter what.

How can you not believe you're meant to be with a guy when that happens? How does anything make sense anymore, when that happens and then he turns out to like boys?

"HE IS NOT!"

"I swear it," I say. I would hold up my hand and do the Boy Scout honor pledge but I am too sad, too tired.

Emily, my best friend that isn't Dylan, has lost the ability to close her mouth. It hangs there and hangs there. Finally, I reach over and gently shut it for her. She blushes, flops onto my bed, and covers her face with her hands.

"I'm sorry," she says. "It's just . . ."

"Unbelievable," I say. "Bizarre? Horrifying? Ridiculous? Ludicrous? Humiliating?"

"Yeah," she says and moves her hands away from her face. "Yeah. But, you know, it kind of makes sense."

Anger wells up inside of me. I push it down to my piggy toes. It does not stay there. "What's that supposed to mean?"

"Well, he does sing show tunes, and he dresses really nicely."

"All men who sing and dress well are not gay!" I yell at her. "That is a stereotype."

She sits back up. "I know. I know. Oh, you poor baby."

She scooches next to me and hugs me sideways.

"I thought he loved me," I sniffle.

She nods.

"I can't believe he doesn't love me."

"He still loves you, honey, just not that way," she says and gives me a little squeeze.

I groan. "Yeah, right."

She thinks for a second and says, "Who's going to help him with his economics homework?"

I shrug.

"And who's going to help him study for English?" she asks.

"I don't know! Maybe me. Maybe we'll still be friends."

We sit there for awhile and then I say, "It must be awful hard for him."

"What?"

"Being gay."

Emily nods. My cat, Muffin, jumps on the bed and rubs her head against our backs. Emily picks her up and kisses her nose. "Oh, who's the pretty kitty. Yes. You are. Yes, you are." She settles Muffin in her lap. "At least he doesn't have some weird cat fetish or something."

"True," I say. "But what if he gets a boyfriend? What if he starts dating someone and then everyone realizes that my quote-unquote One True Love likes boys?"

"That would suck," Emily says. "Definitely. But this is Eastbrook, everyone's going to figure it out eventually."

She picks up Muffin and kisses her kitty belly. Muffin puts her paws on the top of Em's hair but doesn't scratch it. Em moves the cat away and says, "Eddie Caron will be happy."

"Oh, great. My life's goal is to make Eddie Caron happy," I say.

Em shrugs. "It'll make Tom Tanner happy."

"Give me a break. Tom is a shallow, shallow boy who

went out with Mimi Cote and obviously is not my type. He calls me Commie."

"He's liked you forever," she says, settling Muffin back on her lap. "Remember in fourth grade when he gave you that I LOVE YOU ring for Valentine's Day and how jealous Dylan got?"

"That was fourth grade. I'm not really looking for another boyfriend right now." I flop down on the bed, squeeze my eyes tight so I don't cry.

My mother's voice careens down from the living room. Now that she's done with the groceries, she's dusting and singing, which would be embarrassing if it was anyone other than Em here. Em is used to my mother. She's even used to the way my mom sings the wrong lyrics to songs all the time.

"Live like Yoda's crying," my mom sing-yells.

Em starts laughing. "Oh my God, is she screwing up the words to '*Live Like You Were Dying*'?"

"Yep," I say.

"That's so funny," Em snorts. "Does she really think those are the words?"

"She's always stunned when I tell her she's singing things wrong," I say and fortunately for all of us my mom turns on the vacuum and we can't hear her singing anymore. I try to relax onto my bed. "I feel selfish for thinking about myself. I should be worrying about him, you know, all he has to deal with."

"No way. That's his job. You worry about you. That's okay. As long as you only do it for a week."

Muffin pounces on my stomach and knocks the air out of me. "A week?"

"Yeah, any longer and you become annoying, self-obsessed, like a Mallory."

A Mallory is a girl who only thinks about, talks about, knows about herself and how herself reacts/responds/is involved with boys, makeup, clothes, parents, herself.

"I will never be a Mallory!" I yell and sit up straight again, holding Muffin against my belly so she won't run off. She squirms.

"That's right. You are a good Maine girl who gets on with her life," Emily says, raising her hand and putting her fingers in the form of the Boy Scout pledge. "Swear it with me. On my honor, I swear, under God, blah, blah, blah to never be a Mallory."

I raise my hand. I swear. I raise Muffin's paw, make her swear too. Emily grimaces, checks her nails, shakes her head, and says, "You're losing it. That poor cat."

She grabs Muffin, who climbs onto her shoulder and settles there. They both seem to purr. She pulls out her digital camera and snaps a picture of me, even though my nose is red from crying and my hair is a mess. She's always taking pictures ever since her dad died. She's afraid of losing people, afraid she'll forget things about them, if she doesn't snap what they look like happy, sad, angry, bloated from eating too many buffalo wings. She says she can't remember how her dad looked except for how he looked smiling. So, I let her take her pictures and think of how brave she is, how brave I should be.

"A week?" I ask Emily.

She nods, checks out the photo but doesn't show me. She snaps another one of my lonely Gabriel guitar, leaning against the wall. Em throws her sexy brown supermodel hair behind her cat-free shoulder. "A week."

AFTER EM LEAVES, I YELL to my mom that I'm going out on my bike.

She looks up from her computer. She's paying bills and her hair's flopped out of her weekend ponytail, looking all scraggly in her face. "It's cold out."

"Yeah."

She has worry stuck behind her eyes the way she always does when I go out alone, but she's a good mom, she knows that I hardly have seizures, that they don't run my life and she wants me to have a life. "You have your cell phone?"

"Yep."

I kiss her on the top of her head and she wraps her arms around my trunk. "You bundle up, okay?"

I pull away. "I promise."

She smiles and something shifts behind her eyes. It turns out it's a memory. "Do you remember when you were little and you and Mimi Cote rode bikes all the way out to the Washington Junction Road and you both got flats and that guy, Pete, from R.F. Jordan picked you up and put your bikes in the back of the dump truck?"

I clench my teeth. I hate thinking about Mimi Cote. We used to be good friends when we were little and then kind of friends in middle school, but then she went out with Tom Tanner and everything changed. "Yeah."

"You ever talk to Mimi?" my mom asks, but she's already turning back to her computer screen filled with check numbers and deposit statements.

I don't even think she hears me when I say, "No."

I take my bike out and ride until my mind is like the blueberry barrens—this nothing field full of rocks, scrappy bushes, and dried-out fruit. Old footprints in the sand. Abandoned blue jay feathers. A worker's gray t-shirt soaked with sweat.

I know that beyond the barrens is a world of forest with sloping trees, limbs reaching toward the sky, birds flittering from nest to home, to nest. I know that beyond the barrens is a world with nice subdivision houses full of wagging-tail dogs and happy kids, comfy beds, family photos on walls featuring smiles and laughs and hugs, magical stories of love and hope, and refrigerators full of chocolate milk and good leftovers waiting to be rewarmed.

I know, I know that it is all out there, beyond the barrens, beyond my mind and when I ride my bike up and down the Maine hills and around the potholes, over the frost heaves, all I can do is think about wanting, wanting, wanting.

Each want puffs out with my cold breath, making a cloud in the frigid air. Each want stomps itself into my heart as I pedal harder and faster.

I want a life that I can trust. I want a life where there are four stable walls and the people I love are who I expect them to be. Is that too much to ask? I want no one to know about Dylan and me. I want it not to be true.

----o----

Before Emily or Dylan could drive, we all used to walk home from school to Dylan's house, because he lived the closest, only a mile or so away. Dylan would laugh at Emily and how girlie she could be sometimes, quoting from *Cosmopolitan* or *Vogue*. We would all crash in Dylan's kitchen and scarf up all the food in the house, usually bagels. We always ate bagels and tea.

Dylan always made my tea perfect, the way I can never make it. It would come out tasting like apples and cinnamon, not too strong, not too wussy weak like I make it. He'd put the perfect amount of honey in it, stirring the spoon around and around in the mug, without ever clanging the edges. Now, there's no one to make me tea anymore.

Now, he'll be making some handsome boy tea, and they'll kiss each other the way we used to kiss each other, soft and then hard, aching and then fulfilled.

My heart throbs and my feet stop pedaling, because my lips will no longer be the kissed lips. My feet stop pedaling because really where do I have to go? I am in the middle of a road that winds through a blueberry barren.

I was wrong. It is my heart that is the barren, not my head. My head is a river rushing, rushing, rushing and not knowing where it's going. My head is a river rushing, rushing, rushing and looking for the home, looking for the ocean.

----0----

There is nothing to do except go home and hide in my room, stare at Gabriel the guitar leaning against the wall, try not to think about music, try not to think about him.

My mom knocks on my door.

My arms hug my yearbook to my chest and I close my eyes, hoping she won't come in. Hoping never works. The door squeaks open and her voice squeaks after it.

"Honey?" she asks. "You okay?"

I nod, but do not open my eyes.

She says again, "You okay?"

I nod but the nod is a lie and I do not want to be one of the liars so I make my tongue put air out of my mouth. The air forms a word. The word is no.

She rushes in, because that is the kind of mom she wants to be. She rushes in and launches herself onto my bed. Her arms wrap up me and the yearbook in a hug.

"Oh, honey? What is it? Do you want to tell me?"

I shake my head.

She smoothes down my hair with gentle hands. "You sure?"

The volume of Barbra Streisand's voice gets lower. My mom must have turned it down. Dylan's song voice slips further and further away.

I shrug. The thing is, I am really mad at Dylan. I am really mad at him but it's not because he's gay, it's because he pretended not to be. How can I tell my mom that? How can I tell her that the boy she thought I'd marry never liked me that way at all?

She hugs me and rocks me back and forth. "I'm here for you, you know. I'm right here."

"Yep," I say. "Thanks."

I lean away from her. She moves the hair out of my face. It's wet from my tears. Her voice comes out a murmur, "Oh, baby. I am so sorry you are so sad."

I sniff in. "Yeah, me too."

"Okay. I'll give you some space, but you know if you need me . . ."

"You'll be right here," I finish for her.

"I haven't heard you play today," she motions toward Gabriel. "Maybe that would make you feel better."

I shake my head.

I don't think so.

"My fingers are too cold," I tell her. "Maine is too cold."

WHEN YOU SIT ALONE IN your room, hugging your pillow to your chest and listening to pretty cheesy music because the love of your life has turned out to be gay, some pretty simple questions bounce around in your brain over and over again.

Questions like:

How long did he know?

How many times did he kiss me and wish I were a boy?

How many times did he groan inside when I kissed him?

How could I not notice?

It is a completely Mallory thing to hug your pillow to your chest and let your cat crawl all over you while you obsess about things, but I do it anyways and I start to remember one time last week. He came to my house after school. He held my hand walking up the steps and he had such sad eyes. He took my backpack off my back and said, "It's too heavy for you."

I laughed and said, "It's a heavy, heavy burden."

And he said, "We all carry heavy burdens."

I didn't know if he said that because of my seizures, which I hate thinking about, ever. Since I rarely have them, but then I thought maybe he was talking about himself, Dylan.

His eyes were sad but I made it all jokey, because I couldn't stand to see him looking sad, not my golden boy, not my Dylan. I wanted to press myself into him and take all his sadness away, but I also wanted to be inside of him somehow and be that sadness in his eyes, to be tall like him and golden like him, able to sing out those music breaths forever. All of a sudden, I was scared of being me and Dylan being Dylan and I just wanted, just wanted for us to be together, mingled souls like in the bathtub. Or else I just wanted to be a tiny, tiny girl who could disappear into his hugs and not have to see his sad eyes, not have to see them looking at me but not telling me anything.

Tom Tanner drove by and honked his horn. There was a bunch of soccer players in his truck. He waved. I waved back. Dylan's eyes narrowed. He's never liked Tom, since freshman year, although they were best friends in grade school, then Tom went out with Mimi Cote and everything got all weird.

Mrs. Darrow yelled to us from the front door of her house, "I've got cookies if you two want some."

"Thanks, Mrs. Darrow," I yelled back.

We ran over and took a plate of cookies. Mrs. Darrow makes the best cookies. She asked Dylan about his parents and his brothers. She thanked us for raking up her leaves, which we always do, every year, but she always spends the rest of the winter thanking us.

When we walked away, Dylan said, "You ever feel like everything you do, everybody knows about?"

"There are no secrets in Eastbrook," I said and added a hideous movie ghoul laugh and reached my hands out like a zombie's. Dylan's mouth twitched but he didn't quite smile.

He walked behind me into the house like he was protecting me from the whole world outside, a knight in shining armor. He shut the door behind us and locked it.

"Did you take the key out?" he asked me because I am forever leaving keys in the doors. Dylan always tells me it's because I'm so brilliant, because my mind is thinking about so many big things it forgets to focus on the little ones.

I don't feel brilliant now, crying on my bed with my headphones on. I feel stupid and blind and empty, an unused guitar. I feel like someone who has no idea who anybody is.

I wish I still had some of Mrs. Darrow's cookies. What would she think? She always said, "Such a beautiful couple."

Then she would pinch both our cheeks.

----o----

"You look sad," I said to Dylan that day, when we walked into my house with Mrs. Darrow's cookies and the memory of Tom's truck horn vibrating in our heads.

He shrugged. "We all have burdens."

I held him against me and he held me against him and he smelled. He smelled like pine trees and Christmas. He smelled like green earth ready to farm on. He smelled like the wind.

We made love that day. We made love most days and then I'd help him with his homework. But I remember that day best because afterwards he kissed me on the nose, like I was his baby and he traced my collarbone with his finger and said in his husky voice, "I will always love you, you know. Always."

33

"Me too," I murmured.

He grabbed my hand and held it tightly in his. "I mean it."

"Me too."

I will, Dylan. I am so mad at you for being a liar, but I will. I will always love you. I am mad at me for that, too.

- - - - o - - - -

He was just a boy and I was just a girl and that's how it was for a long time. He was just a boy and I was just a girl and he would write me notes when he was bored in class and I would read them and carry them around in my pocket. Then I would write him back. And he would write, "Can I come over this afternoon?"

And we both knew what that meant. It meant, "Let's sing silly songs, play a little guitar, and make love at your house on your bed while your mom's at work." It meant, "Let's lie on the front yard and stare up at the sky and imagine things." It meant, "I love you and I want you and I love you."

I didn't know it was a lie. How could it have been a lie?

I DECIDE TO TAKE A more practical approach and open up my laptop and begin a list on what to do and what NOT to do.

Muffin glances up at me. She jumps onto my desk and knocks over this elephant figurine Dylan bought me once at a yard sale. It's supposed to be good luck if you point the trunk at the door. I point the trunk at the door, give Muffin a couple of strokes, and start typing.

Tips on Having a Gay (ex) Boyfriend

1. Do not tell anyone.
2. Do not call yourself a fag hag, as this is a derogatory term that conjures up Paris Hilton impersonators, Liza Minnelli, and far too much blue eye shadow plastered on a face that has been dried out from one too many highballs.
3. Do not whine for over a week, but during that week explain profusely that a mere seven days is not a sufficient amount of time to overcome the reality that your whole entire identity has been stolen, that your faith in the world has shattered.
4. Wonder why being a girlfriend was your identity. Listen to kick-ass rocker girls who don't give a shit about anything.
5. Think about being a lesbian.
6. Reject the whole lesbian idea when even the concept of kissing super-beautiful Angelina Jolie doesn't make you hot.
7. Wonder how you could have had such good sex so many times with a gay seventeen-year-old guy.
8. Cry.
9. Cry more.

10. Hug your cat. Resist calling him. Resist telling your mother. Resist the whole idea. Resist. Resist. Resist!!!!

11. Decide you must be punked. Look around for Ashton Kutcher, that guy who does the practical joke show, then remember you are not famous and therefore not worthy of being punked.

12. Remember how he looked at that guy selling pretzels at the Bangor Mall. That was not a straight-guy look. Straight guys do not let their eyes linger on other guy's bottoms, unless there is a KICK ME sign plastered there. There was no KICK ME sign.

13. Think about taping a KICK ME sign to your own bottom.

14. Cry.

15. Make a stupid list that does not make you feel better, but gives some semblance of non-hysteria and complete control.

16. Rip list up.

17. Do homework with radio blasting.

18. Give up and go ride bike out to the country. Again.

19. Write him notes. Rip them up, too. Rip everything up so that everything is like your heart, shredded.

I print out my list, because I always print them out. If they're good enough, or important, I thumbtack them onto my corkboard. I call Em again.

"Getting dumped on a Saturday sucks," I say. I print out my tips.

"Uh-huh," she says.

I continue over her, "Because when you get dumped on a Saturday you have all day Sunday to obsess over it and then you have to worry about telling everyone at school on Monday about it. And you know, I'll have to tell people over and over again and everyone will be all shocked that we're broken up."

I pause for breath, pick up my printed-out sheets, and glance at them.

Em inhales so sharply I can hear it on the phone. "Belle, you can't tell people about it."

"Oh God, I can't, can I?" The papers in my hand shake. "Dylan has to tell people."

"Yeah."

I close my eyes. Muffin rubs against my face, moving the phone in my hand. I steady it.

"Why does he have to be gay?" I say. Em doesn't answer because there is no answer. I know that. I know that, but I am acting stupid. "People will notice though. They'll notice when we're not kissing each other all the time, and when we're not together."

"True. And all that butt-groping stuff he used to do."

"My butt is going to be lonely."

"Your butt will be just fine. If anyone asks just tell them that you broke up. Don't give out details," Em's voice is calm, smooth.

"Everyone always wants details," I say.

"It doesn't matter. This isn't about everyone. This is about you and Dylan. Okay?"

I drop my list, pull Muffin onto my lap. "Okay."

```
E--------3-----3-----------------3---------|
A--------3-----3-----------------3---------|
D--------------0---0-   Monday   --0---------|
G--------------0---2-----------x-----------|
B----------------x------0----3-----------|
E---------------------3-------x-----------|
```

Monday

EMILY DRIVES ME TO SCHOOL in her little red car that's the color of a fire hydrant. She knows I don't want to talk so she puts in the soundtrack to *Phantom of the Opera*. This is what we do when one of us is sad. We sing really off-key and really badly in these fake opera voices with super large, exaggerated arm movements.

It usually works, but this time I just watch her out of the corner of my eye.

She's super skinny, Emily is, with no breasts to speak of, but bigger hips than I have. We wear the same size, two, but have entirely different bodies. I look like I outweigh her by twenty pounds, but it's really five.

"It's all in the boobs," she always says. I always nod. She always smiles.

Even now, she's smiling.

"I've got Paddy on!" she shouts at me, even though she's only one foot away in the driver's seat. That's how loud the music is.

That's what she's named her padded bra, Paddy.

"And how is Paddy?" I ask her.

"Sad. He needs some girls to comfort him!" she brakes hard and comes three inches from the tail end of a big orange Hummer. It belongs to our local veterinarian. She just laughs and yells, "Sorry, Dr. Lasko!"

Then she pats my knee. "You okay? Where's Gabriel? Did you leave Gabriel at home?"

Her eyes register a sort of shock like I've forgotten to put on a shirt or something.

"No talking," I tell her as she steps on the gas again. "Just singing."

She nods and starts riffing into a super-high soprano voice. Her nose sticks up into the air and her mouth opens wide, wide, wide.

"Lala LA . . . the Phantom of the Opera!" she screeches. She pulls out her digital camera and snaps a picture at me with one hand. The other hand, thank God, is still on the steering wheel.

Em started taking pictures a couple years ago when her father died. He had cancer. Em used to get annoyed with her mom whenever they were on vacation together because her mom would always wander behind them, taking pictures of everything, so that they could remember it. Now Em's really glad she has those pictures, rolls and rolls of pictures of her and her dad doing anything and everything. I wish I had all those pictures of my dad, but he died when I was so young, just three. I don't really remember him at all.

Emily is always taking pictures. It's her thing. You have to tune it out in order to deal with her, but today I can't.

"No pictures," I say like a movie star. She takes another one and puts her camera between us by the stick shift.

"Fine. Sing then."

She starts off again. I join in. "Oh . . . la something, something . . . The Phantom of the Op-er-a . . ."

"Ahh . . ." she yells going higher, up to an E above high C.

"Ahhh . . ." I sing/shout it with her, making my arms wide open and smacking her in the ear. We screech to the G. "AHhhhhh . . ."

It is like screaming and it feels so so so good.

She hits the REPEAT button on her CD player and we sing it over and over again the entire way to school. We sing it past Dead River Oil Company, and Mike's Store, past Tom Tanner's house, past the library and Denny's. Our voices are hoarse like we both have laryngitis, but our hearts feel ready for what the day might bring.

"That," she says, "is the cheesiest song ever."

"It's what makes it so good," I adjust my seat belt. "The Cheez Whiz factor."

She smiles. "Let's do it again."

- - - - o - - - -

In the parking lot, I stop walking. The high school waits big and cold. Dylan is in there. Will he be waiting at my locker like he normally does? I gulp.

Emily throws an arm around my shoulder. "Come on. Let's go take the bull by the horns."

"The what?" I ask.

She shrugs. "The bull by the horns. That's what my dad always said."

I giggle and start walking forward, shaking my head.

Emily trots after me. "What? What?"

"The bull by the horns," I mutter.

"What?"

"Like Dylan's the bull and his penis is the horn," I snort.

Emily shakes her head at me as the first bell rings. "Oh, Belle. You are not doing well. You are not doing well at all. You've lost it, totally lost it."

She grabs at her bra strap. "Do you want to wear Paddy today? For support?"

That makes me just laugh harder. I yank open the door to the high school and walk smack into Tom Tanner. Tom's in my German class and on the soccer team. He's chestnut color like acorns and good toast.

He grabs my shoulders to gain his balance. "Whoa! Commie, slow it down."

I shake my head. "Sorry."

He seems thrilled to see me and keeps his hands on my shoulders. Then he realizes what he's doing, I think because his eyes shift. Emily lets out a low whistle.

He smiles, a slow smile that would melt an ordinary girl's heart, but I am not into soccer boys who once went out with Mimi Cote no matter how cute a soccer boy he is. He keeps smiling anyways. "It's okay."

Then I remember. Tom Tanner told me not to go out with Dylan, back when we were sophomores. What had he said? He said, "He does more to his hair than you do, Commie."

Tom calls me Commie because I am in Amnesty International and Students for Social Justice, and also because in seventh grade when we did our big United Nations project we all had to be countries and I had to be Cuba, which is a communist country. Tom, of course, was the United States. But that's not what I care about now. What I care about now is how Tom Tanner knew and I didn't.

"Where's the guitar, Commie?" he asks me.

"Home."

He lifts an eyebrow and then gives me a wave and saunters down the hall. I just stand there staring until Emily tugs at my arm. "We're going to be late for Law."

I whirl around on her. "Did everyone know? Did everyone know except me?"

She knows what I'm talking about. Her face scoots down an inch and looks sad.

She sighs and says, "I don't know, Belle. I didn't. Maybe Tom did. I don't know. I mean, they used to be friends in grade school. Maybe something happened."

WHEN I GET TO MY locker, Dylan isn't waiting for me like normal. My head leans against it, feeling the cold, hard metal.

"Belle," says a voice.

It isn't him.

It's Emily.

"We're late," she says.

So I slam my jacket in my locker right next to Dylan's sweatshirt, right above the bumper sticker that Dylan gave me that says "GIVE PEAS A CHANCE." The world seems to swirl and I'm so mad but I don't know at what. At peas? I yank off the bumper sticker, crumple it, and hand it off to Em who knows better than to say anything. Then I throw in my pack, take out the stuff I need, and I go. I go. I go.

I go away from Dylan.

That's what I have to do isn't it?

Sunday was the day of rest, of grieving. Monday is the day of new beginnings. Monday is the day of work.

"WHAT WILL I DO WHEN I see him?" I ask Emily.

She shakes her long, long hair. She gives me worried eyes.

She says, "I don't know."

I REMEMBER WHEN EDDIE CARON caught his girlfriend, Hannah Trudeau, in his truck the first week of junior year. Eddie had been totally in love with Hannah, always holding her tiny, little hand when they walked down the hall, even carrying her books and her lunch tray, completely spoiling her. I'd tease Dylan about how much better Eddie treated Hannah than Dylan treated me.

Dylan had raised his eyebrows and said, "You want me to carry your lunch tray? That's so fifth grade."

I shrugged.

"You don't even get a lunch tray," he said and then he tickled me and then I tickled him back and that was that. But, I always thought it was sweet of Eddie to take care of Hannah like that, to always open doors and give her flowers. My mom called him an old-fashioned boy. Dylan called him a cretin.

But all that ended when Eddie rushed out to his truck after school that day and saw Hannah with her tongue down Ashleigh Martel's throat. Both their shirts were off. He yanked her out and her skinny, little body fell onto the parking lot. Everyone started running over to see what was happening because she and Ashleigh were screaming and only wearing bras, which got all the guys interested and then Eddie Caron was just hauling into her, slapping her and kicking her. She looked so little and Eddie is so big. He's always been big, ever since kindergarten when I used to share my Oreos with him and he'd give me a piece of his beef jerky.

Never in my whole life could I have imagined Eddie Caron beating up a girl. But he was. He just whaled on Hannah.

I screamed for him to stop. I screamed and handed my gig bag to Em who would keep it safe. I jumped on Eddie Caron's back and tried to make him stop but I couldn't because he was too strong. I just clung onto his back like a stupid first grader, shouting at him to leave Hannah alone. I didn't feel anything, not scared, not worried. I was a blank slate, a white piece of paper, an unstrummed guitar, background music.

Tom and Shawn Card hauled him off, yanked him by the arms and bullied him next to the truck, trapping him, cornering him like you do with a wild dog that smells meat and is scared and tastes blood in his mouth. I slid off his back, watching, wondering what to do. Em snapped a picture and I whirled around at her, angry. "Em. No pictures!"

She bit her lip, tucked her camera to her hip. "But it's so good."

She shot me an apology look and started snapping away again. We looked at the pictures later. Ashleigh tugging at her bra strap, stomach flab flapping over the sides of her jeans. Hannah tear stained, red faced, aching against Ashleigh's side. Eddie, my old protector boy, his calm face twisted with wild-dog rage. Tom and Shawn with their arm muscles popping out, restraining him.

Hannah scurried off with Ashleigh but they only made it a couple of feet, clutching their shirts before they just sort of stopped and stared, and someone, Jacob Paquette, I think, yelled, "Dyke!"

Em took a picture of him, too. His mouth wide open and his teeth pointed out his hate.

And Hannah started sobbing. Her tears mixed with blood pooled on the gravel. Ashleigh, though, she had balls. She just turned around, gave everybody the finger, and shouted, "Leave us the hell alone!"

Dylan and Emily came over to me then. Dylan hugged me and said, "You okay?"

"Yeah," I said, but I was shaking and Dylan knew it. Dylan knew I was shaking. So he just hugged me tighter. Then he let go and said, "Everybody's got a right to love."

I shook my head and said like an idiot, "But she was cheating on Eddie."

Now, I know she was too scared to tell. Is that how Dylan felt? Was he too scared to tell? And what changed? Why now? Why be brave now?

Brave. That's what Tom said I was that day.

He came up to me after Eddie calmed down and stomped off. Dylan and Emily were getting in her car, but I was lagging behind, mostly because I was annoyed at Em for taking pictures, and for Dylan sitting on the sidelines, instead of helping me stop the fight. Dylan's best friend, with the unfortunate old-man name of Bob, yelled to him, waved his sax at him. Dylan hopped out of the car and trotted over, telling him what happened, I guess.

I stared at the two of them talking, so different. Bob

so broad and Dylan so sleek. Bob with his too-thick glasses and his too-short hair and Dylan looking like he just stepped out of an underwear ad, only minus the tan.

Tom stood in front of me all of a sudden, blocked my view, and said, "Commie. You were really brave."

It startled me. Mostly because I didn't expect Tom to talk to me without teasing me, which is all he'd done since Dylan and I started dating, but also because he told me I was brave. Dylan never said that to me. Dylan never told me I was brave.

I shrugged like it was no big deal, like I wasn't shaking and he reached out and touched my elbow. His fingers heated my skin. He nodded at me and said, "No. Really, you were. Everyone else was just standing there watching."

"You weren't."

He smirked. "Not in the DNA."

I must have given him a look because his smirk turned into a full smile, he picked at a patch of duct tape on his sleeve and he said, "The whole cop dad thing."

Tom's dad is the Eastbrook Police Chief, which everyone knows, but I never think about it since I don't have police run-ins every day.

"Oh," I said. "Right."

That's when Dylan came back and smiled at Tom but Tom didn't smile back. He just shook his head at Dylan, then winked at me and walked away.

"What was all that about?" Dylan asked while we scrunched into Emily's car.

"Nothing," I said.

"He so likes you," Emily said in this stupid singsong voice.

Dylan's head jerked up and he reached for me from the back seat, leaning forward, wrapping his arms around me, he said, "You're mine, Belle. You're all mine."

Tom knew, didn't he? Somehow he knew.

WHAT IS IT WITH BOYS?

What is it with me that I can't ever tell if they're gay or not?

"Your gaydar is broken," Emily announces.

We hunch forward, whispering over the cafeteria table. I have not seen Dylan all day and I think he's avoiding me, because I mean, it's not *that* big a school. Usually at lunch we sit with a lot of people, but Em and I have asked our friends to give us a little alone time and because all our friends are decent and can tell something is up, they respect it and leave us alone.

I roll my eyes to make my next sentence dramatic. "My gaydar doesn't exist."

"Maybe it's under warranty," she laughs, pulls a drag of Coke into her mouth when she's done chuckling.

"Expired fifteen years ago," I say and moan.

I have spent two long high school years dating and being in love with a gay boy, my best friend, Dylan. My eyes keep glancing over at the boys at the soccer table. Tom Tanner's there, laughing, fiddling with some duct tape, drinking soda. He's got this smile that cracks his face, a superstar smile and when he laughs he throws his head back and his smile gets even bigger.

When we were in eighth grade, I had the biggest crush on him. I was a flyer on the cheerleading team then, and every time my bases put me up into a torch, I would stare at him on the soccer field and will him to look at me. Sometimes he did. Sometimes he didn't, but I always wanted him to. Then Mimi Cote asked him out and they'd always be making out at the dances. I quit cheering after that. I couldn't stand being near Mimi anymore.

I make my eyes go back to Em. She bites the edge of her lip and prepares to ask the question everyone wants to know. She sputters at first but finally gets it out. "Didn't you have any idea . . . I mean . . . When you did it?"

I glare at her.

"No."

Her hands fly through the air. "I mean . . . he must have given you some sort of indication."

"NO!" I yell and some nearby freshman stop eating their pizza and bagels and stare at us. We smile and wave like beauty pageant contestants. I lower my voice and say, "No, everything was in proper working order."

She shakes her head. "That's what I thought. I mean you could tell he had a hard-on and everything whenever you guys danced."

I shrug and lean back to sit up straight and say in a normal voice, "Probably friction."

"He *was* in show choir," she says.

"I know."

"And he does use more hair products than you do," she adds, chomping on a French fry.

"Tom said that too."

"Tom?"

"Back when Dylan and I first started going out."

"Those are stereotypes though," she says, grabbing

another fry. "I mean he's also really hunky, doesn't speak all high and stuff, has a studly boy walk, eats cheeseburgers all the time, and he watches football. You need to eat."

"Yeah." My food is untouched. I haven't been able to eat since Dylan's announcement on Saturday, two days ago. All I do is drink Postum. "Stereotypes are stupid."

I leave Emily alone at the table and go through the lunch line to grab some hot water. It's meant for tea. I don't drink tea unless Dylan makes it for me. It's too mealy, too watery, too nothing, but he makes it workable somehow. I can't drink coffee because caffeine gives me seizures, and even in decaffeinated coffee there's enough caffeine to push me over the edge and start me shaking on the floor or babbling about dogs. That's what I do when I have a seizure, according to eyewitnesses like Dylan and Emily and my mom. I walk aimlessly saying things such as, "The dogs? Where are the dogs? They're barking. The dogs are barking. We have to get the babies."

It isn't the most fun, coherent stuff and I always come off looking like a mental case, I'm sure.

So, I drink Postum.

I flip the hot water on.

Someone comes into the line behind me and makes a little, male, a-hem noise.

Behind my shoulder, Tom Tanner smiles at me. I smile back because my mother raised me to be polite and then his eyes go wide.

"The water . . ." he says, reaches over my shoulder

and flips it off, just before the boiling liquid overflows my insulated cup and attacks my fingers.

The water waits right at the top. I'm afraid to move.

He nudges himself next to me, wraps his fingers around mine. They shoot warmth all the way into my shoulders somehow. I try not to giggle and he says, "We dump it on three. One quick motion. One. Two. Three."

A flick and it's over. He smiles at me. A dimple on his left cheek creases in.

"Thanks," I mumble, embarrassed. My fingers are hot and quivering beneath his.

He moves his away and shakes his head. "You're out of it today, Commie."

I brush some hair out of my face with my stupid, trembling fingers and start over again, turning away so that I don't have to look at him. "Yeah. I know. I didn't get much sleep last night."

"Out partying?"

"Yeah, that's me. Sunday night party girl."

I flick off the hot water, way before I have to. It's barely half-full.

"Studying for German?" he asks.

"German?" I close my eyes and groan. He laughs.

"You forgot about the test?"

I nod.

"You, Belle Philbrick, forgot about a test?"

"Don't rub it in," I tell him as he fills up a cup with yummy coffee, caffeinated. Jerk.

He shakes his head. "That's got to be a first."

My empty stomach makes room for my heart, which is sinking lower and lower in my body. Tom must notice because he puts his hand on my shoulder and says, "Belle, everything will be okay."

"Yeah. Right," I mumble like a bratty fourth grader.

"With the test. With Dylan. With everything," he says. His hand weighs against my skin. "I promise."

Then he drops his hand and turns away, leaving me with half a cup of water, another fear gnawing away at me, and a monster headache and a question. How did he know?

"No guitar today?" he calls over his shoulder.

I shake my head, confused. He's asking about my guitar. I always bring Gabriel to school. Didn't he already ask me about this? Didn't he already ask about Gabriel? Maybe he's just trying to keep talking. I have no idea why, though.

"I forgot her," I lie.

He nods and keeps walking.

How did he know about Dylan? How did he know?

I STOMP AFTER HIM. HE sits with the soccer guys, Andrew, Ben, Brandon, Shawn. He's making some sort of miniature alligator out of duct tape while the other guys watch.

"Cute." I put my water down on the table and stare him down.

The other guys start chuckling and Shawn goes, "Uh-oh, Tommy's in trouble."

Tom doesn't move.

"How did you know?" I ask him.

He looks away. He looks at the soccer guys. Andrew gulps down his Coke.

"Know what?" Tom says.

"About Dylan. About me and Dylan," I demand. My heart threatens to pound out of my chest. I wonder if Tom can see it beating. I wonder if he'll catch it.

He raises his hands up. "Belle, um, now's not a good time."

"Just tell me, Tom."

"Yeah, Tom," Andrew says all snarky. "Tell her."

Andrew grabs Tom's duct tape alligator and makes like he's biting Tom with it. Tom bats him away.

I wait.

"Belle . . ." Tom swallows hard. His Adam's apple moves down his throat. He extracts himself from the bench.

I glare at him. Andrew uses the alligator to bite his own throat. All the guys laugh except Tom who stares back at me as hard as I stare at him. Finally, he grabs my shoulder and walks me to the Coke machine. Ian Falvey, a freshman, is there, trying to get a dollar bill to go through, but it keeps getting rejected. Tom hands him some quarters and says, "Scram."

The kid puts the quarters in, grabs his Coke, and throws a "Thanks" over his tiny shoulders.

Tom leans against the machine. He watches me fume with my hands on my hips.

"Belle," he sighs out my name. He shakes his head. "You're mad at the wrong person."

"I'm not mad at you," I pull in a deep breath trying to calm down. "Just tell me what you know."

Tom tilts his head toward the ceiling. He moves it back down to meet my gaze. Nothing comes out of his mouth.

"Tom, just tell me." I'm ready to throttle him. To pull the words out of his mouth with my hands. I try to be civil and say, "Please."

But instead of sounding civil, my voice sounds weak. It sounds like breaking, like a fairy flower figurine that's been knocked over by a dog's tail, like a teddy bear that's lost a leg during a rambunctious slumber party and because Mimi Cote likes to play keep away, like a heart of a girl who doesn't know what's what anymore, like breaking, breaking, breaking into pieces and trying not to.

"Please." I beg him.

"I shouldn't be the one who tells you this. Dylan should tell you this." He grabs me by the shoulders to steady me, and then moves me behind him so I'm between the Coke machine and the wall. He's hiding me, I think. He's hiding me, because he doesn't want the world to see me, the stupid girl, the Harvest Queen with the gay-boy king. For a moment, I wonder, maybe Dylan is in love with Tom and that's how he knows. For some reason this crushes my heart against my spine even more than the thought of Dylan just being gay. What if Tom is gay too? They used to be best friends. They hate each other. Maybe that's it . . . Maybe every guy I've ever lusted after is gay. My face scrunches up. I refuse to cry. I stare at Tom right in the eyes, an alpha-dog stare.

He licks his lips. He swallows. "I saw Dylan kissing Bob. I know something's going on, okay?"

My mouth falls open. The Coke machine rumbles next to me. I lean against it. Not Tom. Of course, not Tom. Bob. Bob. Kissing Bob.

"Belle?" his voice says. It comes from far away, down a long, long tunnel that I don't want to go into, but what else can I do? Dylan is gay. He kissed Bob. There is no going back, the entire fairy tale life I thought I had has already been revised, the song I thought I was singing has moved into a different key and there's nothing I can do, nobody I can get angry at. It's just gone. It never was.

"Belle?"

"When?" I make my lips move. "When?"

"Yesterday, at the mall. In the parking lot."

Yesterday, they were kissing while I was listening to

Barbra Streisand, or telling Em. Yesterday, they were kissing while I was wondering how my life could have fallen apart, staring at his picture, trying to keep my heart beating, my lungs taking in air. Yesterday.

I close my eyes. The world wiggles beneath my feet. I open my eyes and try to focus on Tom's face. It's so far away, so funny looking. I blink away my tears. I rub at my chest, trying to erase all my anger. Instead, I crumple.

"Oh," I say. "Oh."

Tom wraps his arms around me and someone nearby whistles.

Tom wraps his arms around me and I let him. I crumple. There is nothing else to do.

----o----

Tom pulls me into his arms, then he settles me on the floor.

"You okay?" he asks.

"Did I shake?" My voice is frantic. I couldn't have had a seizure. I've had no caffeine, no aspartame, nothing. All around me, people stare, but I don't feel fuzzy brained like when I have one. Oh God. "Did I shake?"

Tom's confused. "What do you mean? Shake?"

"N-nothing," I stutter. I swallow; try to calm down. "What happened?"

He brushes some hair out of my face. "You fainted. You were out for like three seconds."

I struggle back up, but Tom's not letting go of me. He thinks I'll fall again, I bet. "I do not faint."

My cheeks turn bright red.

He smiles, and there's a swagger in his voice as he says, "What would you call it then?"

I think. My hands raise up in the air. "Passing out?"

He laughs some more and the soccer guys all come over, which makes me blush worse. My cheeks feel like they are on fire. They start teasing him. "What did ya say to her Tom? Finally ask her out?"

Blah. Blah. Blah. I tune them out, but I watch Tom. He smiles but his eyes are pained. He smiles but his hands shake a little like they do when he has to give an oral report in German.

"It's my fault," I laugh. I try to save him. "I got dizzy. Tom was doing his knight-in-shining-armor routine."

I bat my eyelashes, but it makes me feel a little woozy and I sway. Both Tom and Shawn grab me and Shawn yells, "Whoa!"

By now, the whole cafeteria's looking and Emily's run over with her hands over her mouth. She knows I'm horrified that I'll have a seizure in school. She knows it's unlikely to happen in school. It wasn't a seizure, though.

"Did you forget to eat? Girls always forget to eat," Andrew says. He's still holding the little alligator.

"I bought some Postum," I explain.

"What's Postum?" Andrew asks Shawn.

Shawn shrugs and says to me, "I'm getting you some food."

He takes off and Emily bursts in, grabbing my arm where he let go. "She hasn't eaten since Saturday!"

I shoot her a death-beam look.

"She's not anorexic or anything," Emily blurts. "She's . . . she's just stressed about Dylan. They broke up."

I give her super-laser-beam eyes. She covers her mouth again.

Tom raises his eyebrows. He mouths the words, "So you knew?"

I shrug, but Emily's seen the whole thing and she says out loud, "He told her Saturday night."

Tom's back goes rigid. He shakes his head. "That's crap."

"What's crap?" Andrew asks, looking clueless and silly in his soccer shirt. They are all wearing them. There must be a game today. "What's crap?"

"Nothing!" I tell him. "Just how stupid I am passing out. What a weenie. Ha?"

I stand up, push away the helping hands, stagger over to Emily, and try to look like I've got it all together. Even I know I'm failing miserably. Shawn comes hauling ass over and he's got a bagel in one hand and a grilled cheese in the other.

"I didn't know what you'd want," he says and he looks so sweet and little, like a four-year-old boy who has made his mommy a picture, even though he's more like six foot eight and could have sex with every single cheerleader in school.

"Thanks," I say. "That's sweet."

"Ooo, Shawn is sweet," Andrew croons and bats his eyelashes.

Shawn turns red. "Better not let Dylan hear that."

The silence sinks into all of us, even Shawn, who still holding the food, lifts his hands in the air and says, "What? What did I say?"

Emily grabs the grilled cheese for me and pulls me away, back toward our table, but not before I hear Andrew pantomimes the alligator saying, "Shawn, buddy, Dylan is no more."

Tips about Postum

1. Postum is the elixir of the blue-hair set. Even brand new cans look like they come from the 1950s. There's a dried-up label with old-fashioned block-style lettering that says, "Postum, Instant Hot Beverage. Original. Full-Bodied Taste. Naturally Caffeine Free."

2. Postum mixing is an exacting experience. If you submerge the spoon into the hot water, the brown grains adhere to the metal becoming a brownish sludge reminiscent of dog diarrhea. I do not ever think about what it does to the lining of my esophagus and stomach. Some things you are better off not knowing.

3. You must tip the spoon, wait a moment, and then stir. Do not think about passing out in front of the cafeteria. Do not worry if it's some new kind of seizure.

4. Sip and enjoy the combination of water, wheat bran, wheat molasses, and maltodextrin (from corn).

5. Fend off the curious who gawk and say, "What the hell is that?"

6. Hide beneath the cafeteria table and finish your drink away from the demanding crowds.

THE FIRST TIME I EVER had a seizure was right after I started dating Dylan. We'd been just hanging out in the family room in the basement, watching *Survivor,* this reality show where they live in nasty places and vote each other off and whoever wins gets really skinny from only eating maggots, and they also get a million dollars. I was drinking my 509th Pepsi of the day and he was snarfing down nachos.

Somebody on *Survivor* was crying because she missed her husband and Dylan snorted. "God, what wusses."

I started to agree, but the Pepsi can in my hand was shaking. I tried to put it down. But then my fingers let go. They straightened out all rigid and shook, shook, shook and I opened my mouth to say something but before I could, I was gone.

I woke up with my head in Dylan's lap and Pepsi all over the floor.

"Dylan?" I was totally confused.

He kissed the top of my forehead. "It's okay, Belle. You're okay."

Everything in my body hurt like I'd run a marathon. My head looped around against itself. I started to cry. "What happened?"

Dylan shook his head. "I don't know. I don't know, sweetie, but I'm right here. I'm right here for you."

"You swear?"

He nodded again. "Swear."

- - - - o - - - -

But he won't be anymore. He won't be and I can't handle that. I want to hide. It's like everyone in the whole cafeteria is staring, staring, staring at me. Em keeps talking, trying to pretend like everything's okay, but it isn't. It isn't at all.

"I've got to get out of here," I say to her.

"What?" she cocks her head. "The bell's going to ring in like two minutes."

I gulp the rest of my Postum and then I just get up and take off out the cafeteria door. I slam past everyone at a speed-walker pace and then sprint across the parking lot, heading toward the softball field. I race so fast that no one can stop me.

When I left, Em stood up and yelled my name. I hope no one heard her. I hope no one saw.

Tom saw though. Tom sees me now and he runs faster on those soccer legs. He grabs hold of me behind the old green dugout, by the words EASTBROOK ROCKS. We've both escaped the high school lockup, sprinted in school clothes (me) and soccer uniform (him) past everyone and everything, past gray walls with scuff marks on them, past linoleum floors and people's concrete eyes, past the stares. Now, we're out here under the big sky, with our backs against the dugout, barely panting, just a little.

"Life sucks," he says to me.

I can't say anything, just wipe my hand against my face, which is all wet from tears and sweat. I can't tell which is which.

"Life sucks and then you die," I mumble.

He coughs out a laugh. A squirrel chitters at us from the top of the dugout. We've invaded his space.

My back slides down the dugout wall. My bottom plops on the cold ground. My legs turn to straight sticks in front of me. Dylan told me they were pretty legs. I choke on my own breath and start to sob, just sob, because there isn't anything else I can do.

My shoulders shake. My eyes turn into mountains releasing all the melted snow, turning it into rivers that cascade down my shirt, puddle into my hands and lap.

Tom leans me toward him. His arm wraps the straightness of my back, wraps itself around me. When all the snow has melted, I wipe my face with my hands. I look away at a softball, white, fat, round, stuck in a puddle full of leaves, forgotten and abandoned during some game last spring. I feel like the softball, but I'm not. Or maybe I am. I'm a softball and Tom's the puddle I'm stuck in. No. Tom's a leaf in the puddle with me, waiting to see what will happen. The puddle is my own tears.

"I'm sick of crying about this," I say, wiping at my face.

He lifts an eyebrow and says in a real cranky way, "Have you cried about it a lot?"

It's not like I've been a Mallory, really, completely crying and feeling sorry for myself. "I just mean, I'm tired about crying about this right now."

He nods and his fingers drum against my shoulder. "It's okay to cry. It sucks."

I nod my head. "Yeah."

The squirrel pelts down two acorns at us, one after the other.

"Grumpy little guy," Tom says.

"Me?"

"The squirrel."

The squirrel leaps from the edge of the dugout to a pine branch that swoops out near us. He rushes up toward the trunk, turns around, and scolds us again.

"I don't feel like I know who I am anymore," I tell Tom, and once the words rush out of me, just like a hyper squirrel's chatter, the truth of them hits me hard in my stomach. I stare at Tom's face, this teasing guy, this ex Mimi-flame. "Why am I telling you this?"

"You need a friend, Commie."

"I have friends," I say. A logging truck zooms by on Route 1, past the baseball field, heading to Bangor and points beyond. Maybe Canada. Maybe Boston. Maybe to a tanker that will take the lumber to Japan or Russia, somewhere exotic, somewhere not here. "I'm not a Commie."

"You know that, then, don't you?" Tom says. He pulls me closer and jostles me around in that brother way of his. The squirrel chucks another acorn at us. It hits my foot. Tom turns serious. "I think, that sometimes when you're with the wrong person, you try to become what that person wants. You lose yourself and who you are, just a little bit, but that doesn't mean you can't get it back."

"Like Dylan with me?"

He shrugs. "Yeah. Or me with Mimi back in eighth grade. But I was really talking more about you with Dylan."

We don't say anything. The squirrel calls over a friend and they scurry up and down the branches, angry, worried over their acorn stash. Who do they think we are? Acorn-stash abductors?

Tom pulls his leg up close and fiddles with some duct tape that he's pressed on the side of his shoe. In tiny black letters he's written a line.

"'Exit, pursued by a bear?'" I ask.

"It's a stage direction in *The Winter's Tale*."

"By Shakespeare."

"Yeah."

"I wouldn't figure you for Shakespeare."

"What would you figure me for, Commie?"

"I don't know," I reach out and touch the duct tape with my finger. "Soccer? I mean if you're going to quote something on your shoe, I guess I'd imagine soccer."

He doesn't answer.

"Do you always quote people on duct tape and smack it on your shoe?" I ask.

"Sort of."

Tom smells nice like marshmallows on a campfire and we sit there for a good, long while, annoying the squirrels by our very presence, before I say, "We're going to get in big trouble for this."

He fidgets with some duct tape on his sneaker, pulling it off, tearing it in half, folding it in and out. "You think the squirrels will send the rodent mafia after us for invading their territory? Maybe in the middle of the night we'll be cozy in our beds only to be besieged by chipmunks wielding hand guns. Exit, pursued by a squirrel."

"No," I laugh and bop my shoulder against him before I remember my newest worry. "In school. We just raced out of school."

I imagine detentions, suspensions, getting kicked off National Honor Society. I imagine our principal stopping my mom in the produce aisle of Shop 'n Save, telling her what a bad kid I've become. Is that who I am? A bad kid? I shudder. The squirrel chucks an acorn at us, right toward my face. Tom's hand flashes out and he catches it before it hits my cheek.

"I'll talk us out of it," he says, slowly opening his fingers to reveal the acorn resting in the middle of his hand.

I turn to stare into those brown eyes of his. I don't know how to look at him when he's not teasing me. "You can do that? You can talk us out of it?"

"Commie," he says, giving me a fake gentle punch on the chin. "I can do anything."

I nod at his sneaker. Duct tape is wrapped around the sole of it, like a bandage. That piece doesn't have writing on it.

"You're into duct tape, huh?"

"It can do anything," he smiles, stands up, offers me his hand, then offers me the acorn.

"Kind of like you, right?" I kid and grab the acorn. It's a Tom shade of brown, rich and homey.

"Yeah, kind of like me," he says, but he's not kidding at all.

Since I don't stand up, he comes back down to me and we sit there for a little bit longer and the wind blows against us so hard we have to huddle next to each other. My fingers turn blue. Tom says, "You remember in eighth grade when you used to cheer at our soccer games?"

"Yeah," I say.

"I liked that."

I narrow my eyes at him. "You liked Mimi Cote."

He shrugs. "Only cause I couldn't have you."

"Couldn't *have* me?" I raise my eyebrows at him. The wind whips a twig against my legs. I reach out and start stripping it of bark, but it's hard to do because my fingers are so cold. "Why couldn't you quote-unquote have me?"

"Dylan and I made a deal."

I snap the twig in half. "Really?"

"If you or Mimi asked one of us out, we'd have to go out with them, leave the other one alone," Tom shakes his head, does his little half-smile thing. "Mimi asked me out."

"That's awful, like we were prizes or something," I spit out.

"It was eighth grade."

"It's completely stupid," I yell at him. He puts his arm back around me and sort of jostles me the way a big brother would do. I try to edge away, but it's too much work, so I stay put.

He nods. "Yeah, it was stupid."

LOOK SORRY. ALL I'M SUPPOSED to do in the vice principal's office is look sorry, Tom says.

That's not going to be hard. I am sorry.

I'm sorry that I'm such an emotional idiot.

I'm sorry that I passed out in the cafeteria.

I'm sorry that I only ate half that grilled cheese because now I'm super hungry.

I'm sorry that my face is death girl white with red splotches on it that match the rims of my eyes and I have to walk through the halls looking like this.

I'm not sorry that I ran away though. I'm not sorry about that at all.

WHEN WE ARE FAR ENOUGH away from the principal's office, Tom and I give each other high fives.

"Told you I could do it," he says, smiling huge, showing all his perfect white Chiclets teeth.

"You were awesome," I tell him.

He smiles even bigger, raises his hand for another high five. When I slap it with my own hand, his fingers grab my own fingers. "You know what this means, Commie?"

I shake my head. My fingers tingle. They must be numb.

"This means we're partners in crime," he says.

My eyebrows raise. "Like Andrade and Trevi? Like Burke and Hare or Bonnie and Clyde. Like Cuba and the Soviet Union back in the 60s?"

He squeezes my hand, drops it, and crosses his arms in front of his chest. "Commie, sometimes you're too damn smart."

I wish, I think. I wish. I wish. I wish.

OKAY, DYLAN. I'M SITTING HERE in advanced biology looking at a dead pig. Emily and I are trying to find its spleen, but it's proving to be a little more elusive than we thought. If I'm in bio it means you are in chorus, with Bob. With BOB!

I need to talk to you about things. I need to talk to you, but I'm afraid to even see you. I'm afraid if I see you it will rip my heart into pieces, that it will feel like a scalpel jabbing into the center of me.

Emily is currently using the scalpel to cut through some abdominal muscles in her quest to find the spleen. She keeps wrinkling her nose and saying, "Disgusting."

I don't think she'll find the spleen.

I don't think we ever find anything, do we? I mean in life. I mean we think we find things and then it turns out those things aren't what we thought.

How could you not be what I thought?

In my pocket, again, is the note you gave me last Friday.

You wrote, I just want to be free with you. Just like that song "I'm free" on the Cold Spring Harbor tape. You made me free. I think that's part of the reason I like you so much.

What was that supposed to mean?

Our science teacher, Mr. Zeki, has given up on us.

"You can't find the what?" he shrieks at Emily.

She is pointedly trying not to stare at the crotch area of his too-tight chinos. I know this because she told me this is often a problem. When he struts up to our science-lab table he always stands on the Emily side and his genital region is pretty much the same level as her nose.

She fidgets with her fingers. She puts her hair behind her ear. She fidgets with her fingers some more.

She seems to have lost her gift of words. I evilly wish this had happened in the cafeteria when she told everyone about the state of Dylan's and my relationship. Then I feel guilty for having such a thought, so I bail her out. "We can't find Pamela's spleen."

Mr. Zeki's eyebrows raise. "Pamela?"

I cough. It feels like the whole science room's listening. "Um. Yeah. Pamela. We named our fetal pig Pamela after Pamela Anderson, the actress with the really big, um . . ."

Em's face turns the color of roasted ham. Anna, who is at the lab table in front of us, starts laughing.

So does Mr. Zeki. He recovers quickly. His too-tight groin area shifts closer to us, our pig, and Emily's head. "I see. Let's see if Pamela has a spleen, shall we? Or maybe her other endowments have taken over her entire anatomy."

The class laughs. Emily puts her head in her hands. Pamela just sprawls there, waiting for the exploration.

----o----

"I hate Mr. Zeki," Emily says later.

"Me too."

"I know we have an above-normal quota of freaky teachers here, but he's the worst."

"No, my German teacher is the worst. He dresses up like a woman," I say.

"I'm glad you're okay," she says, slamming books in her locker and pulling out her gym clothes. Emily has PE last period. I have German. "I was really worried about you at lunch, and then when you ran out."

I shrug. "My mom would say I've become unstrung."

"I know I didn't run after you, but I thought that would make it even a bigger deal and Shawn said Tom would take care of you, that he's good at stuff like that. Breakdowns and stuff. Must be because his dad's a cop. Tom took care of you, didn't he?"

I shrug again and lie, "I did not have a breakdown."

Emily looks at me, really looks at me, wipes my growing-out bangs away from my face. "It'll be okay, you know. You still have six more days of whining."

I try to smile but I can't do it. "Think I'll make it?"

Emily grabs my shoulders and gives me a little shake. "Yeah. Yeah. I think so." She fumbles her camera out of her duffel bag and as she snaps a picture of me, her tiny sports bra drops out of her bag onto the floor and some idiot sophomore boys start pointing and laughing. She scoops it up, hauls out her middle finger, and waves it at them. She turns to me and says with a big sigh that hits all of her, "Me? I'm not so sure."

----o----

Because I've been dreading German I walk really slowly down the halls. It feels like everyone's staring at me, whispering about me and Dylan, me and Dylan. People like Rachel Austin and Callie Smith say hi and ask how I'm feeling, and I know that today I am in the hot topic in the Eastbrook High School hallways and in the notes everyone passes each other instead of listening to the teacher, and don't forget all the text messages.

"Did you hear Belle Philbrick passed out at lunch?" Katie Vachon says to Travis Bunker as I walk by. "She and Dylan broke up."

"Did you hear he's gay?"

"No way," Katie says. She used to have a crush on Dylan. We run spring track together. I used to think she was nice, until right now.

"Yeah-huh. Somebody saw him kissing a guy with no hair at parking lot of the Bangor Mall."

"Wow."

"Double wow."

"She booked it out of there, too."

"She fainted?"

"Swear to God."

"Mimi says she's totally mental."

I ball my hands into fists and wonder if they think I can't hear them.

Shawn passes by and says, "Hi."

Some people nod.

Some people turn their heads away. Some people turn their hearts away. Some people turn, turn, turn.

Totally mental.

Some people like Rosie Piazza ask me how I'm doing, if I'm okay.

"Yeah, I'm okay," I say. "Thanks."

Dylan isn't the only one who knows how to lie.

----0----

I slip into my chair, hoping no one will notice me. Tom's desk is right behind me, but I don't look at him. I'm afraid to look at him. I'm afraid to look at anybody in here, but there's one person I really want to look at. There's one person I want to stare with x-ray-vision eyes, just stare and stare and stare and ask him, "How could you?"

I want to grab him by the shirt and haul him up out of his chair like I'm one of those ripped action-movie stars. I want to beat him over the head with a guitar until they both splinter into pieces on the floor. I want to haul his squat butt up and say, "How could you? How could you? He was mine!"

But that was never true, was it? He never was mine.

He always belonged to himself. He always belonged to Bob. I just didn't know it. I didn't know anything.

"Guten Tag, Belle," says Mr. Reitz, Herr Reitz we're supposed to call him.

So much for being invisible.

"Guten Tag, Herr Reitz," I say real low, so I almost can't even hear myself.

He saunters up to me and smiles. He's wearing lederhosen today, which is better than when he wears his clown outfit or dresses up like a female opera singer. That means we'll be doing Beatles songs in German. You can always tell what the lesson plan is by what Mr. Reitz wears. First, though, he decides to torment me.

"Was habst du letztes Wochenende gemacht?" he asks.

What did I do this weekend? I slouch down lower and say the only thing I can remember in German right now.

"Ich habe im Atlantik letztem Wochenende geschwimmen." I swam in the Atlantic. It's a lie, but it's better than, "I found out my boyfriend was gay, passed out at lunch, cried for hours, and wished I could die."

Herr Reitz, always the actor, grabs his arms and shivers. "War es kalt?"

Yeah, I tell him, it was really freaking cold. "It was so cold that the chickens were lining up at the KFC, begging to jump into the pressure cooker."

That throws him. That throws everyone, and Herr Reitz bends over, clutching his lederhosen-clad stomach. I let myself smile.

When he finally rights himself he says, "Can you say that in German?"

I shake my head.

"You don't have to. That was too funny. Somebody write that down!"

Then he goes back into German Teacher Mode, moves on to Bob and asks him the same thing, "Was habst du letztes Wochenende gemacht?"

Bob flinches and behind his glasses, his twitchy little eyes look at me. His twitchy little eyes look at me and it's all I can do not to get up and pound him. Behind me, I can hear Tom let out a breath real, real slow. I grip the edge of my chair and will myself to be still.

Herr Reitz waits for Bob's answer.

We all wait for Bob's answer.

"Ich habe gesungen," he says.

I sang.

ONCE WHEN EMILY WAS DRIVING us to one of his jazz choir concerts I asked Dylan about it, about why Bob was always hanging around him but never around us.

"He's shy," Dylan said.

Emily and I gave each other looks and he leaned in from the backseat, his voice all emphatic.

"He's got a lot of baggage," Dylan said. Em turned down the music. "His mom has multiple sclerosis."

We knew that. Everyone in Hancock County knew that. Bob's mom used to be the band teacher, but she had to retire early because of her MS. There were all sorts of fundraising concerts for her. Dylan and I both performed in them. Still, Em nodded, all sympathetic. I stared out the window feeling evil, but I wouldn't let it go.

"He looks at you funny, just hangs around you," I said and I wanted to say, eating up your popcorn words and your sing me songs like I do. Like I do.

Dylan put his hand on my shoulder. "He just needs a friend. We've always been friends."

"But why can't he hang out with all of us?"

Em took a picture of us then. Dylan's face all twisted and angry and me angry and sad and stupid all at once.

"Don't get all hyper about it, Belle. It's not a big deal," his hand left on my shoulder. Em snapped off another one-handed picture and swerved. "I'm just helping him out. Is that some sort of bad thing?"

I shook my head. I wiped my eyes with the back of my hand. "No, it's not."

I want to know. Do they make music together? Does he play the saxophone and does Dylan sing and is it sweeter than it was with me? Is it a bebop melody or a lullaby?

Our test is translating lyrics to German songs.

The universe is tormenting me.

The songs?

Love, Love Me Do
She Loves You
Eleanor Rigby . . . the one that has the line about lonely people and how they are everywhere.

Across the aisle, Bob hums under his breath. It sounds like a mosquito that roams around your head when you go to bed at night. It sounds like a pin pricking the tips of your fingers over and over again. It is hard not to throw my Deutsche text book at him. It is hard not to scream.

Finally, finally, finally, Tom says, just low enough for Bob to hear, but not loud enough to alert Herr Reitz, "Shut up, Bob."

Rasheesh, who is about four feet tall and a wicked brat goes, "Yeah, Bob, shut up. You sound like a drugged-up black fly."

Bob stops for maybe two minutes and then he starts up again.

It's about loving someone do and always being true.

I break my pencil in half.

Top Ten Reasons Why I Can't Believe I've Been Dumped for Bob

1. He hums during German class.

2. His glasses are thicker than the soles on L.L. Bean hiking boots.

3. He smells funny, like mothballs or something, mixed with metal.

4. He hums BEATLES songs in German class.

5. He's in band.

6. He scratches his head too much.

7. He hums BEATLES songs in German class OFF-KEY.

8. He wears tighty whitie underwear that show his butt because his pants are always doing that working man's smile thing on him.

9. He hums BEATLES songs in German class OFF-KEY and taps his FEET in time.

10. He's a boy.

THE BELL RINGS. WE GRAB our books. I fold up my list and shove it in the bottom of my shoe, to remind me why I'm mad, and that it's okay to be mad, even if I'm supposed to try to love everybody and all that Students-for-Social-Justice stuff. Bob skitters out of German class but he pauses at the door. He turns around and walks back, walks toward me, one step, two.

"Belle?" his voice cracks.

I keep gathering my books, but Tom's turned still, standing at my elbow like some sort of protector dog.

"Yeah," I say to Bob. "What?"

"I'm sorry," he says and he turns and runs before I can say anything back. My words, my emotions are peanut butter stuck somewhere behind my incisors. *He's* sorry.

Tom comes up behind me, puts his hand on my shoulder, and says, "I have a game but I can run you home if you need a ride."

I shake my head. "I've got a Key Club Meeting."

"Pinko Commie," he says and scruffs my hair like I'm a black lab or something.

"Takes one to know one," I bounce back, but it sounds flat. It doesn't sound like our normal teasing. "And 'pinko'? What's with 'pinko'?"

"That's what all the fascists used to call the communists. Pinkos."

"So, you're a fascist?"

"No. Jesus. That's not what I'm saying," Tom's eyes

drill into mine for a minute, like he's trying to figure things out and he finally says, "You still playing guitar?"

"Yeah. You know I play guitar." Everyone knows I play guitar. I bring Gabriel to school every day, and lots of time I just skip out on most of lunch and go play her in an empty classroom, but maybe Tom's just making conversation about something he thinks is safe so I shrug and think about Gabriel, lonely, stuck against the wall of my room, soundless.

"You didn't bring it to school today," he smiles behind his hand, which was scratching at his cheek.

"You've told me that, what, twice now?" This is a little snarky, but I don't care. "I mean, it's not like I'm attached to my guitar, like she's some sort of security blanket or something."

He shrugs and I feel bad for being snarky. "You were good at the talent show last year."

"Thanks."

He smiles and turns away and then shouts over his shoulder, "For a pinko commie."

THERE'S THIS LITTLE CEMETERY UP the road from my house, all hidden by trees. The tombstones have sunk into the earth. Moss and lichen mar their whiteness. Time flattened away the names on the stones.

Dylan and I would go there sometimes, when we wanted to be alone, when my mom was home. Or sometimes we'd just walk down there when we wanted some quiet. We'd hold hands and duck our heads between the low cedar branches, inhale the sweet smell of woods coupled with silence, and slip between the granite pillars that once held a gate, I guess.

We'd wander among the gravestones.

"Charlotte Block," Dylan said. "I bet she had an affair with the good reverend, and pined her days away, looping together rugs from scraps, the maiden aunt in the corner, misunderstood, empty but for her longing."

I squeezed his hand and then squatted by Charlotte's grave. "Too sad. She married young and had lots of babies. She wrote poems about ferns and kittens playing with mice. She tried to be who everyone wanted her to be, but never succeeded."

"She tried so hard to be what was expected that she lost herself," Dylan added.

I sighed and pulled him down next to me. We leaned on Charlotte's grave. His tan calf rested on the ground, touching mine. The sun had lightened the hairs on his leg to a gold color. It sparkled against the grass. It was so much bigger than my leg, despite all my biking. He still had bigger calves.

"Do you think everyone's like that?" I asked him. An osprey flew over us, circling, searching for something on the ground while it soared in the air. "Hey, an osprey."

"It's beautiful," he said. We stared at the v-shaped markings on its wings. "Yeah, I think everyone's like that."

"Everyone's trying to be someone they aren't?" I plucked up some grass and split the blade in two.

"Yeah. To different degrees, but yeah."

The grass fell from my fingers. It hit Dylan's knee. I brushed it off. "Even you?"

He nodded. The osprey circled higher, farther away. "Yeah. Everybody. You too."

The air heavied against us. I swallowed. The osprey shrieked. "I don't want to make you into someone you aren't."

He shook his head and he put his arm around my shoulder, leaning me into him. "We do it to ourselves. It's scary to be who we really are."

"I don't think I'm trying to be anybody I'm not."

He let go of my shoulder and leaned away, obviously annoyed. "Belle. Give me a break. You don't think you aren't trying to live up to other people's expectations?"

"Well, yeah."

I grabbed a handful of grass and started sorting it on my thigh, separating the strands by lengths as Dylan kept talking. "When are you happiest?"

"When I'm with you," I leaned in and kissed him. He sighed and gently pushed me away.

"Other than that."

I pouted and then decided to answer. "When I play Gabriel."

He nodded, excitement flushing his face. A squirrel twittered at us from a nearby tree. "Right. But you don't play it all the time. You don't even expect to do it for a living, do you? You're going to be a lawyer, right? Why's that?"

I grabbed the grass blades off my leg and scattered them. I didn't answer. I hated it when Dylan did this psychobabble stuff. I loved that he was smart and philosophical, but I hated when he used it on me.

Up in the sky another osprey joined the first one. I wondered what we looked like to them, two tiny specks on the ground, too big to eat, but small, small, small in the scheme of things.

Dylan answered his own question. "You don't think of being a guitarist because that's not what's expected of you. You don't sit around playing guitar all day because that's not what other people want you to do. You change your own wants to fulfill other people's expectations."

I stood up. "Like you don't."

He kept sitting there, sad taking over his face. All my anger melted away. "No, believe me, I do."

----o----

Sometimes we would try to memorize the names of the people in the cemetery, the names of the people whose stories are long gone, who are invisible now, the unremembered.

We would chant them like a mantra, with our eyes closed.
Our voices overlapping each other.

Larry Rohan
Charlotte Block
Frances Block
Ebenezer Block
Cpt. John Mortan
Horatio Alley
Elizabeth Alley

"We should make up songs about all of them," I told Dylan,
propping myself up on my elbow so I could see his face.

He kept his eyes closed. "Why?"

"So people will remember them."

"Who'll make up songs about us?" He opened his eyes.
They were grainy green, like they had texture and depth.

"We'll make up our own songs," I said, kissing him
lightly on his lower lip. "Deal?"

He nodded and closed his eyes again. "Deal."

- - - - o - - - -

When we were walking home, I stopped and wrapped my
hands around him.

"You should be who you want to be," I whispered.

His hands tightened on my back.

"I can't."

"Sure you can," I said and then to lighten the mood I
licked his ear.

He hollered and chased me the entire way home.

At the Key Club meeting, it is decided that we will sell bracelets at the YMCA's Middle School dance to try to raise money for a gym at the Hancock Consolidated School. This girl named Gillian was killed in Hancock last summer by a car. She'd been riding her bike. There aren't any shoulders on the roads in Hancock. It's a dangerous place to ride a bike. Gillian was big into sports and she would have come in to our high school this year, because Hancock, like lots of towns around here, don't have their own high schools. Anyway, her parents thought that building the Hancock School a big gym in Gillian's honor would be a good way to make sure that no one will forget her.

It's a good idea. Still, Hancock County's a small place. Nobody will ever forget about Gillian. Her big sister, Anna, is in Key Club, she starts crying when everyone agrees to sell the bracelets.

"Thanks," she sniffs and wipes her big, beautiful brown eyes with her sleeve. "It means a lot."

I tiptoe over and sit next to her and hug her, while everybody else finishes up and Rachel adjourns the meeting. Em clicks a picture of us hugging and Anna gives her the finger.

Em lifts her hands up. "Sorry. Sorry. I don't know when to quit."

Anna groans, smiles, and waves her finger a little bit more, before tucking it into a fist. Em's so cute, everyone forgives her everything. Except for Mimi Cote, who could not get over the time Em took a picture of her leaving the girls' bathroom with the back of her skirt tucked into her thong. You can't really blame Mimi for that. Em says it's all in the name of art. I don't know what kind of art you call it to see Mimi's butt hanging out of a thong, but whatever.

Anna leans over and whispers to me, "I'm sorry about Dylan."

"Yeah," I nod.

She sniffs in again, pushing her long black hair over her shoulder and says, "Is he really gay?"

"Yeah."

Right then, Em's eyes meet mine. I move my hair in front of my face in case she's thinking about taking another picture. My eyes start to tear up. Anna pulls me into the side of her fluffy sweater, her hugging me this time.

"You poor baby," she says. "It sucks to be you."

"It sucks to be a lot of people," I say.

"Yeah," Anna says, letting go of me. Our sad eyes meet. "Yeah."

I try not to call. I want to call. The phone waits and waits for me to cradle it against my face like a long-lost baby, like a lover, like a teddy bear. Gabriel leans against the wall and waits and waits for me to wrap my arms around her and make her sing.

I pick up Muffin instead. She mews but decides it's more comfortable to sit on my shoulder than my arm. Dylan would flip her upside down and hold her like a baby and even though that's got to be an uncomfortable position for a cat she always purred and purred anyway.

She trusted him.

I wait and wait and wait but he does not call me.

He always calls me every night.

It was hard coming home today without him. My bed looked angry at me. It wanted him there. I plopped myself on it, but it wasn't the same. The bed knows that the weight of one is not the weight of two.

In my room, I pull out last year's yearbook from its place on my bookcase.

This is what he wrote in his chicken scratch writing. This is what he wrote.

Belle,

What can I say to tell you how I feel about you? I want something you can remember. I could say I love you, but would you remember that since you're reminded every day. I could say we will get a St. Bernard when we get married, or I could say that you'll make me happy forever. But what would really stand out in your memory?

Our love will last forever!

I think they all go hand in hand, those things I wrote up there.

No, I'm not done and I know I'm slow but I needed something to say to the one I love. Okay. I'll get off your back now.

I love you very much.

Dylan Alley

I want to know why he signed his last name. Did he already know then? Did he know the St. Bernard and the happy forever were lies? Did he know that when I'm thirty or forty I might have not talked to him for decades and even remembering the first letter of his last name would be a struggle? Did he know?

I shove my yearbook under my bed, where Muffin's been sleeping with the dust balls. She scoots out, zips across the carpet, and out the door, abandoning me. I reach under and take the yearbook back and read what he wrote again. And again. Then I try to remember what I wrote in his yearbook. I can't, but I know it was happy, chirpy, something about making music together and singing Barbra Streisand songs forever. I don't even like Barbra. She's so showy.

I clamber off my bed, pull the CD out of the player, and stare at its shiny, perfect circle. My two hands grab each side and that's when I twist and bend the Barbra CD, trying to break it, but I'm not strong enough. Instead, I unlock my window, open it, open the screen, too, and whirl the CD like a Frisbee into the blackness of the night.

"Have a horrible flight," I whisper. "Don't remember to fasten your seat belt. Emergency exits cannot be found to the rear and front."

It's a shiny silver UFO glinting over my lawn and then it drops and it's gone.

- - - - o - - - -

One time we were volunteering at Living History Day at the Black House, helping kids play nineteenth century games, like walking on stilts, or running around pushing a big hoop with a stick. We volunteered because of Key Club, and because the Black House, this museum that was really just a preserved big, brick mansion, always needed help.

I was holding this little girl up on the stilts when this man came and yanked his little boy away from the hoops. He was this stereotype guy, beefy, angry, with hair short in the front and long in the back, a wardrobe from another decade.

"What the hell are you doing?" he barked at the boy, holding his little arm at a wicked angle.

The little girl on the wooden stilts stopped walking across the perfectly manicured lawn and sucked in her breath. I grabbed the stilts so she wouldn't fall over and Dylan, Dylan gave this beefy father guy the evil eye.

The guy didn't notice, just yanked on his son more, pulling at him so hard that the little boy stumbled on his own feet. I had no idea what made him so mad, just that he was mad. The boy fell over and scraped his knee. He started crying.

The dad stood there, hands in fists. Dylan rushed over to the little boy with a first aid kit, washed off his knee.

"Leave him alone," the dad said like a growl. "Serves him right. Such a freaking sissy."

Dylan put on the Band-Aid, stood up, and said, "Sir, he's not a sissy."

The man huffed. "Like you'd know."

Dylan stood up straighter then. I sucked in my breath.

"You want me to prove it?" Dylan stared at him.

I helped the little girl off the stilts and took her hand. She whispered to me, "My daddy didn't want to come down here. We live in Bangor. He's been grumpy all day."

She let go of my hand and ran to where her brother, father, and Dylan stood on the perfectly manicured grass. "Daddy! We should go. We gotta get home for supper."

She grabbed his arm and yanked on it, once, twice, another time.

From behind the house came the splash and screams of someone going into the dunk tank.

The father's posture eased. He nodded. "Let's go."

But Dylan wasn't ready to let it go. He yelled after them, "Children are gifts, Mister. Treat them with kindness."

The man turned for a moment, gave him the finger, and then walked away.

Dylan shook his head and I came up behind him and wrapped my arms around his waist, "I'm proud of you."

He nodded. I could hear his heart thunder beneath his shirt, his skin. "There's no such thing as a sissy."

How could I not have known?

----o----

While my mother sleeps, I wander the house again and stop in the kitchen, open the fridge, pull out the hummus container. In the fridge light, I stand there and I take the knife and spread the hummus on a cracker. Muffin jumps up on the counter and I scream, drop the knife. It clatters on the floor.

My mother yells in her sleep voice, "What is it? What is it?"

"Nothing!" I yell back, scooping the knife up off the floor, into my hand. "Just making a snack. Go back to sleep."

Some sort of combination growl/slumber noise emits from her mouth, while I stand in the light of the refrigerator, caught, knife on the floor, bruise on the heart.

```
E - - - - - - - 3 - - - - - 3 - - - - - - - - - - - - - - - - 3 - - - - - - - - - |
A - - - - - - - 3 - - - - - - 3 - - - - - - - - - - - - - 3 - - - - - - - - - |
D - - - - - - - - - - - - - O - - - - - O - - - - - - - - - - - O - - - - - - - - - |
G - - - - - - - - - - - - - O - - - - 2 - - - - - X - - - - - |
B - - - - - - - - - - - - - - - - X - - - - - - - O - - - - 3 - - - - - - - - - |
E - - - - - - - - - - - - - - - - - - - 3 - - - - - - - X - - - - - - - - - - |
```

Tuesday

Since sleep was not an option last night, I scramble out of the house as soon as it's dawn. I prop up a note by the coffeemaker on the counter: *Gone Riding.* I've put in my mom's required eight-and-a-half cups of water and three heaping coffee scoops of Folgers Hazelnut. That's what she needs before she heads out to work. She'll be all set.

I chug off up the hill with my wheels spinning, wool hat trapping my hair against my head. It doesn't do anything to keep the cold from hitting my teeth. The shrill pain of it is what I want, anyway.

Tom's dad, the police chief, drives by in his cruiser. He honks and waves, then he stops ahead of me and rolls down the window. I stop next to him, wondering if I've broken some sort of bike road rule.

He leans out the window, but he's still got his seat belt on like a good cop. He has crinkles by his eyes that make him look old, but other than that, he's got the same look as Tom: strong, dark, healthy. "Pretty early for biking, Belle."

I nod. "It's the only time I'm free."

"You cold?"

"Yep."

He nods his head and says, "Get in the cruiser for a sec."

I walk my bike to the side of the road, brace it against a tree, and hop into the cruiser. Warm stuffy air blasts against my cheeks. It smells like sugar in here. I try to see if there's any evidence of Dunkin Donuts. Yes! A coffee cup. No donuts, though.

Tom's dad notices me looking, waits a second, and says, "I gave up donuts."

I bite my lip, embarrassed, but he just laughs in such a good, friendly way that my nerves calm down just a little.

"The whole stereotype of small-town cop/big-town gut was too much for me." He pats his stomach, which is flat and lean like Tom's. He takes a big breath and says, "Belle, I didn't call you in here to talk about donuts."

"I didn't think so," I say, trying to keep my calm but I'm wondering why I'm in here. Is he going to arrest me? Yell at me about not dating Tom in eighth grade. I'm wearing my dorkiest bike helmet, pink with pictures of Minnie Mouse riding bikes with Mickey so I'm obviously not breaking that law. I sit on my hands to warm them up and keep them from shaking.

He fiddles with the dial to his radio. I notice his gun on his waist. He's got a police radio on the dashboard, a radar detector, handcuffs. There's a lot of crazy stuff in here and it makes me nervous, even though I like Tom's dad.

He takes another big breath and says, "I heard about Dylan."

Ah, great. It's my turn to take a deep breath. Dick McKenny drives by us and honks. He runs the county ambulance service. We all wave.

"What about Dylan?" I say to buy time.

Tom's dad raises his eyebrows and gives me a look that says he's used to the runaround and has no patience for it. "That he's gay."

He just flat-out says it like that.

"Do his parents know?" he asks me.

"I don't think so," I say, gulping, but if he already knows, maybe everybody knows. I look away, out at the woods. The thick, overgrown, trees lean every which way, worried down from ice and wind. They make everything claustrophobic like the entire town is leaning in, listening. They block out the sky. Sometimes I long for a big sky and no more listening trees, for horizons and no more neighbors knowing your business.

Tom's dad says, "Belle, I know this is hard on you, so I'm going to cut to the chase. Okay?"

I nod, bite at the side of my lip, unbuckle my helmet, and tuck some of my hair back into my ponytail. "Okay?"

He locks me in with those charcoal eyes, just like Tom's. Someone else honks but neither of us look to see who it is, we just raise our hands in an automatic wave. He sighs and says, "I wish you never went out with that boy, Belle. He's a great kid, a smart boy, but not for you. We both know that now, right? When Tom told me what the two of them agreed to back in eighth grade."

"You mean the deal?" I say, smirking.

He nods. "Stupid business. But what I want to say Belle is that they call Eastbrook a city, but with 6,000 people or so, it's really just a town, a small town. You and I both know that."

He looks straight ahead, grabs his steering wheel, bites at the side of his cheek, and says, "You and I both know that some people in Eastbrook aren't all that forward thinking. They might give Dylan trouble. I told Tom. He's going to be on the lookout in case anything happens, but when I saw you riding your bike, I thought maybe I should tell you too."

"What kind of trouble?"

"It was only twenty years ago when those boys dropped that gay guy off that bridge up in Bangor, you ever hear about that?"

I nod. It was horrible. They chased him out of a bar and down the street and then dropped him into the river. He died, of course he died. Just because he was gay. I cringe because I don't even know his name. What if that happened to Dylan? Although, it's hard to imagine anyone chasing him down, intimidating him, he's so strong, but still . . . What if they did and then twenty years later nobody ever knew his name and he was just the gay guy someone murdered. I blow on my hands. I press my lips together. That can't happen.

"Not that anyone's going to drop Dylan off a bridge or anything, but there are some people in this town who think like that, who believe being gay is being evil."

"They're stupid," I mutter like I'm five years old or something.

"Yep. They're stupid. But they exist and Dylan . . . Well, he needs to be careful," Tom's dad taps me on the head. "You're a smart girl, Belle. You've got a good head on your shoulders. I want you to watch out for Dylan, tell him to be cautious, okay?"

I nod and a huge gulp of fear wedges itself in my throat. It's all I can do not to cry, all I can do not to sob in Tom's dad's cruiser, sob and wish it could all go away. I don't. I manage to say, "I'll tell him."

"Good," he nods. "Good. You know, you might want to look for signs of depression too, a lot of boys who are outed in high school get depressed, suicidal."

I whirl on him with big eyes and stammer out, "Suicidal? Dylan? That's crazy."

Dylan's always been one of the most together, happy people I know. He glows. He dances around. He's a star. My Dylan could never be suicidal. I gulp and swallow, gulp and swallow again and then I lean my head back against the seat. Tom's dad pats my arm awkwardly and says, "Not all boys, Belle. Just some. I've asked Tom to keep an eye out for you, too. I know this has got to be hard for you."

"You asked Tom to look out for me?" I say. My words come out slow like they are numbed. My heart presses in on itself for some stupid reason. Of course, Tom was only being nice because his dad asked him to. You can't be mean to poor, pitiful Belle Philbrick, the girl who was so clueless that she didn't know that her boyfriend was gay.

Tom's dad turned down the heat a little. "This is hard on you, too, Belle. You need support."

My heart drops but I nod and wipe at the corner of my eyes and then Brian Barnard, the accountant whose daughter was an all-state basketball guard two years back, drives by in his big black Dodge SUV and honks. We both look at him and wave and smile, but I wonder. Is he one of those people? The people to look out for?

----o----

When Tom's dad lets me go, I ride up hills, down hills, past the cemetery where Dylan and I had our first kiss, past the spot Dylan, Emily, Bob, and I thought we saw a UFO once. We were driving home from one of Dylan's recitals. Bob's mom didn't show up to pick him up so Em brought him home.

I pass houses just waking with sleepy coffee smells, stale breath, orange juice, cinnamon-roll hangovers.

The cold and a fog hangs about the trees, clings to them, shrouding everything in grayness. It's a gray town, a bland nothing town, but if Tom's dad is right it's got little slashes of red fire hiding in there, red-colored hate waiting to burn through the fog.

I ride and ride and my quads start to burn and the sun starts to rise and my heart doesn't ache anymore 'cause it's too busy just beating, trying to pump the energy through my broken-horse body, trying to keep up with the demands for blood, blood, blood.

Then I realize where I am. My hands squeeze the brake pads. The back tires skid on the frozen gravel, but I don't fall over. My feet stomp to the ground, holding me steady.

It's a house, gambrel style, cute white with a big garden in the back, a sunroom in the front and a pool. It's got a camper in the driveway and pumpkins on the front steps that no one's smashed, at least not yet, but it's almost Halloween. There's a St. Bernard on the side lawn, looking at me, not barking, wagging his tail.

Inside this house, it smells like blue paint and beef stew and cinnamon tea. Inside this house, it smells like a big Swedish and Irish family where most of the kids have grown and gone. Inside this house, it smells like love and incense and soil for flowers to grow in.

This house is Dylan's house. I stare at it; stare at his bedroom window with the curtains still drawn. That's not normal. Dylan's usually the first one up, singing good morning like a bird in a tree greeting the day, that's what his mom used to say.

His mom, she thought we'd get married. She'd laugh when I came over and ruffle my hair and say, "How's my future daughter-in-law?"

I wonder how he'll tell his mom. I wonder how he'll tell his dad. I wonder how he'll tell his older brothers. I wonder if he'll get the chance or if someone will tell them first. Maybe they'll learn in a hushed whisper, an angry hiss of hate.

"Oh, Dylan," I say aloud. Only the wind answers me, whistling the leaves, telling me to give it up, to turn around and to ride my bike home. I do.

My mom's up and humming, shuffling around the kitchen when I get home.

"Good ride, honey?" she asks, hugging me hello.

She smells like coffee. I used to love coffee before I had to give it up. Coffee and gum are my addictions. Now I'm a Postum and Tic Tacs girl.

My mom puts my favorite mug, a Halloween ghost mug, into the microwave and presses the minute button and says, "I made your Postum for you."

I slide into a chair, stretch out my legs, flexing my feet to loosen up the aching muscles. "That's sweet."

"You want any toast?"

"Yeah," I start getting up, but my mom puts out her hand.

"I'll do it. This morning how about I pamper you?"

I smile at her and knead my calves. "Okay."

She makes my toast and pulls my Postum out of the microwave.

She starts singing, the wrong lyrics, of course, like she always does. It's this old Led Zeppelin song, *Stairway to Heaven.*

"There's a feeling I get when I look at my waist," she sings as she stirs.

"Mom," I say and roll my eyes. "It goes, 'There's a feeling I get when I look to the west.'"

"Oh," she laughs and smiles and runs her free hand through her hair.

She doesn't have much hair. It's thin and dyed red and

floaty. It's old woman hair really. My mom had me when she was twenty-two, which makes her . . . what? Thirty-nine? She's a bit plump, but she has dimples when she smiles and when she laughs and she likes to laugh. She worked so hard for so long doing the kind of job that would kill anybody's soul, but a couple years ago she got a new job at the hospital. Before, she was the receptionist at this dental supply company. She worked by this cabinet where they have rows and rows of pretend teeth, all different sizes, all different shades from super-star white to tobacco yellow. They use them for caps and dentures. When I was little, I'd have nightmares about those teeth coming after me in the dark, attached to jaws of course, and chomping, chomping, chomping away.

I shiver and just then my mom hands me my peanut butter and honey toast along with my Postum.

"Thanks," I say while she kisses the top of my head.

"You betcha."

She walks over to the counter, sips her coffee, stares at me, and I brace myself for the Mom Moment, the moment when my mother tries to be the kind of mom you see on sitcoms and old tv shows, the Uber-Mater, Herr Reitz would call it, the super mom.

"Is everything okay with you, sweetie?" she asks.

"Yep," I lie, take a bite of toast.

"No seizures lately?"

"Nope."

"Good, I'd hate for you to have to go on that medicine again."

Before they knew what caused my seizures, Dr. Dulli put me on medicine. He tried a million kinds, but something always went wrong. My blood would get toxic, I'd hallucinate. I'd be allergic. Seizure medicine works great for some people, but not for me. That's why we had to try so hard to figure out what was causing them, the seizures.

I shudder, thinking about it. The sweet honey on my toast coats my tongue. All those rashes, all that sickness, Dylan was there for me the whole time.

My mom sips her coffee, creating a calculating silence while I try to hurry down my food so that I can escape to the shower.

"Dylan hasn't called the last couple days," she says.

I shrug.

"Things okay with you two?"

Postum solidifies in my stomach making a good globby pit. I stand up and rush the words out, "We broke up. It's no big deal. I'm okay."

"Oh, honey—"

My mom's arms reach out to me but I'm already gone, past her and fleeing to the shower where no one asks me questions, where no one looks at me with pity eyes.

Mr. Raines, our lovely principal, announces on the intercom that the Boys' Varsity Soccer Team "stomped on Trinity" yesterday afternoon.

Emily snarfs. "Sounds like they took out the father, son, and Holy Ghost."

I'm laughing with her, walking down the hall to first period, when I see him. I see Dylan. Everything stops. My heart stops. My feet stop. My soul stops. Even Emily stops and says, "Uh-oh" beneath her breath, real quiet.

Dylan lifts his hand cautiously. His fingers wiggle a bit in a tiny wave.

"Hi, guys," he says.

"Hi," I say. I scan him. He does not look too depressed, but how does a depressed person look. I have no clue. I say it again, all awkward and stupid, like I've never seen him naked or held his hand or seen him cry, "Hi."

"Hhmm," is all that comes out of Emily's mouth and I can tell by her tensed-up back and the way that she's clutching her books that she's trying to vaporize Dylan with her kitty-cat eyes.

"Belle, I wanted to tell you . . . about Bob . . ." he starts to say. His hands flap around in the air like they're trying to pull the right words out.

Emily grabs me by the elbow, steers me by this golden boy, this sad-eye boy who used to hold me in his arms. She says, "We'll be late for class."

"Yeah, right," Dylan nods. He looks at me. "I'll talk to you later."

I don't say anything. I can't say anything. My heart has gone so big, so haywire that it thumps everywhere in my body. It's taken control of all of me, just thump thumping away. It's all I can hear.

Thump. Thump.

Thump.

Thump.

Finally Emily's voice breaks through as she does a speed-walk hustle through the hallway, "Really, what freaking nerve. Who does he think he is? What a scum bag. He didn't even say anything about you passing out in the cafeteria yesterday, I mean, everybody in the whole school knows about it and he can't even act concerned. Jesus, I can't believe you ever went out with him."

Thump.

Thump. Thump.

Blah. Blah. Blah.

Emily's words are nothing words. All I can think about is Dylan and his gold, gold soul and the way his fingers used to feel against my skin when he touched me.

I turn around and look for him in the hall, but my Dylan has disappeared. Another boy, still golden, stands still as people part around him. He lifts up his hand and waves goodbye.

Em stands next to me, camera in front of her like a gun, she clicks a picture of the hall with the new Dylan in it.

She checks the picture on the viewfinder and shows me, "That's a good one. High school hall. Devoid of meaning."

"Yeah," I say. "Right."

Then I remember what Tom's dad said and I rush down the hall, back toward Dylan, leaving Em standing there with her camera, probably taking a picture of me. I rush past Shawn, Mimi Cote in a stupid metal Mimi-skirt, Eddie Caron. I get to Dylan, watch his shocked, sad eyes and I gush out my words, "You have to be careful, Dylan. It's a small town. Tom's dad said that people might come after you. He wanted me to warn you."

Dylan stares at me. "Tom's dad?"

His mouth is a straight line.

He shakes his head and says, "I'll be fine, Belle."

Then he walks away, leaving me in silence, except for my stupid heart that thumps and thumps, alone.

- - - - o - - - -

Eddie Caron and all his hulking, big glory comes up behind me in the hall and puts his hand on my shoulder.

I jerk away, startled.

We both mumble, "Sorry."

We walk together toward class.

He clears his throat and says, "You and Dylan really broke up?"

"Yeah."

"Saturday night? When I drove by?"

"Yeah."

"For good?"

"Yeah."

He shakes his head. "I never would've believed it."

I shrug. "Me neither."

He bangs next to me. "Sorry. You were too good for him, though."

I whirl on him. "No I wasn't."

"Sure you were."

"No," I whisper. "I wasn't."

He lets the silence nestle between us and then he says, "If you ever need anything, just let me know, okay?"

"Yeah, Eddie. Okay," I say. I stare at this huge man/boy. Back when we were in kindergarten together and we'd hold hands waiting for the bus, he'd build me castles in the road dirt while we waited and say stuff like, "I'll be the knight and you be the princess and I'll protect you."

"No, Eddie," I'd tell him. "I want to be the queen."

He'd nod in that slow way of his and he'd say, "Okay. You be the queen and I'll be the knight and this is your castle and I'll protect you."

He was so sweet, if even an ant came by, he wouldn't squish it. He'd pick it up and move it somewhere else. He's so big now and we are so far apart. I can't even imagine holding his hand. I blink my eyes and for a second wish we were little kids again and everything was easy, and our biggest problem was worrying about getting beaten up on the bus.

He stands there, waiting for me to say something intelligent, I guess, his big brawny body blocking my way into class. He smells okay, though. His eyes are harder than his kindergarten eyes.

I smile at him and say the only thing I can think of, "Thanks."

SEEING YOU IN THE HALL today hurt like hell, Dylan. My breath stopped. I am so mad at you and at the same time, I'm so worried about you. Your eyes were so sad. I can't imagine what it's like to be you, to be gay in a world where gay is dangerous, where gay means being dragged behind a pickup truck or thrown off a bridge or not being allowed to be a scout leader. It's a world where gay means you can die because you've loved.

You're in that world now, Dylan. You're in that world and I'm not. I'm left here, watching, hoping, waiting. I'm left here wondering about how hard it was to be you when you told me, when you loved me, when you pretended that I was your soul mate, life's light, and all that hokey, new-age lovey-dovey stuff.

How hard it must be, Dylan.

But I'm still hurt and I'm still mad, because you were my best friend, you know. You took care of me when I had a seizure or got a B on a test, or yelled at my mom or had a fight with Emily.

We swore that we would always be there for each other, but how can we do that? How can we do that when we are in different worlds?

Why do I keep writing you notes in class? Is it because I used to? What else should I do?

I fold them up into little squares and put them in my left pocket, carry them around all day. They weigh me down. They keep me from floating away to the drop-ceiling roof with the water stains in it. They help me get it out. What else should I do? Tell me. What else should I do?

In my right pocket is the note from last Friday. I put it in my pocket every morning.

You wrote: You don't seem to have a cold anymore. That's great. I love you.

I am afraid to see you. I am afraid of what I might say. I am afraid of what you might say. I'm afraid that you'll tell me that it is true, that you never loved me, that it was all one big, fat, horrible, heart-breaking, ego-shattering lie.

Tom calls me Commie. He should call me Wimp.

An old note falls out of my copy of *Catcher in the Rye*. Go figure.

It's all bent and crumpled and I instantly know what it is. It's the note Emily wrote me the day before Dylan finally asked me out. Dylan and I had been friends forever and he held my hand once during a movie, but that was it. I, of course, had the hots for him. Well, I had the hots for him and Tom Tanner, but Tom didn't call me every single afternoon. Tom didn't have green eyes and he didn't talk about things like souls and God and reincarnation and love and auras. Tom played with duct tape and talked about soccer and he never called me on the phone, even after he broke up with Mimi.

"Mimi asked me to the dance," Dylan told me on the phone when he called me about it.

Hate made me clench my teeth together and grind them. I forced my mouth open to talk but I couldn't breathe. "Mimi?"

"Yeah," he said, chewing something. It sounded like a bagel.

Quiet rested over the phone line. I closed my eyes and put my face in my cat's fur. I counted to ten. I imagined what life would be like with a name like Mimi. Dylan and Mimi. Dylan and Belle sounded better.

"What are you going to do?" I asked him.

"I don't know," he said. I swear I could hear him shrug.

"Well, do you like her?"

A pause. "Not that way."

"Mm-hhmmm."

I could breathe again.

Mimi and I had been best friends until eighth grade. We'd do makeup together, sleep over at each other's houses. Mimi always put stuffed animals in between us in bed to make sure we didn't touch each other, like that was some big awful thing. I did better in school and in sports, but she was a much better flirt.

"Do you like Tom Tanner?" she asked one time at cheering.

"Yeah."

The next day she asked him out. Then she did it again, with Dylan.

Emily and I discussed it all via a note in Algebra II. Emily's handwriting commanded both sides of the page, with its extravagant loops. Mine seemed cramped, tiny, shy. She was stressed about whether to drink at a party. I was stressed about the Mimi situation.

Well, Belle, scared of what?

Of being "in love." If we went out I don't know if we'd ever break up. I mean, I like, love him and I understand him because in a way he's part of me and I him. We're like two souls that are one, but not identical.

That sounds corny.

Well, okay, whether you drink or not is up to you, but don't if you don't want to. And do if you do. If you don't know now decide when the time comes. You'll know what to do. Intuition.

Good advice! Do you believe the saying opposites attract? Because if you're that alike it would be hard to keep the relationship going. See the thing I don't understand is what you want to happen between you two? Understand????!!!

I don't know!
It's just—I know it's like meant to be and stuff, but I have to wait cause to truly love someone you have to work out the things that need to be—and you have to be ready to love them and they you. Do you know?

*That's very philosophical there Belle. But don't you in the slightest want to be dancing in Dylan's arms Friday night or do you want Mimi to be . . .
Tell the truth . . .*

Yeah, but I can't make him love only me and I know he does but I don't know if he's ready to.

Well, suppose you and Dylan were going to get married soon. Would you approve of him having affairs ?!?

If we were getting married, there'd be a commitment and he'd be ready to love me. We're only 15. This is scary for a fifteen year old. You love people in different degrees, anyway.

Yes, I can see that, but first you have commitment to be boyfriend/girlfriend and then you have whatever next in everything, even now.

WHO WAS IT WHO WROTE those words? Some confident girl. Some girl who knew her stuff. Some girl who didn't have a boyfriend, and wanted one, but didn't really need one. That girl was me.

I RIP THE NOTE UP into a thousand pieces, and I don't care that I'm in the middle of English and that Rachel and Mimi stare at me with big eyes and whisper behind their pretty manicured hands. Everyone is, except for the guys. The guys like Andrew and Travis raise their eyebrows, shift their jock legs uncomfortably, the guys like Rasheesh cross their nerd knees, or if they're invisible boys they nod in sympathy.

I don't care. I make confetti, march up in front of Mr. Patrick, right in the middle of his lecture, and flutter the pieces into the trash bin.

Then I raise my hand and answer the next question just to prove how cool I am.

"I don't believe that the thematic impact of Adrienne Rich's poem, 'The Afterwake,' centers around the fatigue mentioned in the second stanza but on the word 'nerves' at the end of the first line."

Blah. Blah. Blah.

Andrew starts laughing and applauding. Kara Raymond does a cat whistle. I sit down and smile. Mr. Patrick shakes his head and says, "I don't know what to do with you, Philbrick."

Andrew mutters, "I bet Tom would."

Mr. Patrick points because he's heard. "Andrew. You see me after class."

I blush scarlet. I wish Em were here. God, I am so stupid.

I understand him, I wrote. *He loves me*, I wrote.

I can't believe I was so stupid.

I can't believe I spent two years of my life loving a guy who is gay.

"I'M DONE WHINING," I ANNOUNCE to Emily as I stir my Postum.

The stupid red coffee stirrer keeps bending. It's not tough enough to slosh around the thicker stuff, the Postum stuff, the hearty stuff.

Emily raises her eyebrows. She sips her Coke.

"I mean it. I'm officially done whining," I repeat. I pull out the stirrer and suck the end.

"Uh-huh," she says.

"You don't believe me?"

"You're allowed to whine a little," she says. She twists the pop top on her Coke. Twisting. Twisting. She yanks it off. She takes a picture of the Coke can, pop topless.

"I'm done whining," I tell her.

My head spins. She flicks the little metal pop top at me. It skitters across the table. I slap it down with my hand, keep it from sliding off the table top and into the abyss of the cafeteria floor.

"I mean it," I say again. "I'm done."

- - - - o - - - -

All during lunch people come up and ask me if I'm okay. Callie Clark gives me a supportive hug. Amiee Ciciotte tells me that I'm better off without Dylan. Shawn comes over 800 times and asks Emily and me if we need anything. She makes googly eyes at him.

My eyes keep glancing over at Tom's table. His eyes glance over at mine and when our eyes meet, lock, and hold it's like electric shocks bounce up and down my skin.

It's crazy, uncontrolled electricity and it makes me scared a bit and my breath hitches and I turn away. And there's this other thing stuck in there too, this thing that gnaws at me. His dad told him to look after me. That's it. That's all. Why does this matter? I have no idea.

When Emily's Coke is gone and my Postum has sunk to the bottom of my stomach, she says, "You know, I'm not sure if liking other guys yet is a good idea."

I lift up my eyebrows at her.

She fiddles with the buttons on her camera. Her unoccupied hands flits through the air with her rapid-pace words. "I mean, it's good in the way that it means you're moving on, right? You're moving past this, which is healthy, but maybe it's not, because it's like a rebound thing, you know? It's like maybe you aren't giving yourself enough time to recover from the trauma of your relationship."

"The trauma of my relationship?"

"Yeah," she nods, sighs, and puts the lens cap on. "You know. It's a big deal, what's happening to you and Dylan and everything. That's hard to adjust to. You loved him for, like, forever and then—boom—that love's gone."

I stare into Emily's blue eyes. She stares back with sympathy. I say as undramatically as possible, "It was a lie, Em. It was just a fairy tale. You don't have to recover from a fairy tale."

She exhales, plucks off the lens cap again, and twirls it between her fingers. "Yes, you do."

----o----

Emily and I head off to science. Just outside the cafeteria door, Shawn stands in front of me, totally blocking the way. His too-big eyes are sad, sad, sad and he stares down at me so intently that I'm worried that there's dandruff on the top of my head or something.

"Belle," he says.

I wait.

He doesn't say anything. Emily fluffs her hair and flutters her eyelashes, totally subconsciously. She's had the hots for Shawn forever.

He stares at me.

I wait.

He clears his throat. "I'm sorry about Dylan."

"Oh," I say and suddenly find my shoes incredibly interesting. They are canvas Snoopy sneakers with clouds on them, arty but cool. Snoopy holds the balloons floating up above his red doghouse, heading up, up, up into a blue sky.

Shawn clears his throat again. "It sucks that he's gay."

I nod because what else am I supposed to do?

Emily coughs and shifts her weight in her bright yellow clogs. Shawn's sneaker taps the floor. Footwear is very interesting these days.

"I didn't know," he says.

"Yeah," I shrug. "Me either."

"Really? You couldn't tell?"

People push by us. Rachel, Mimi, Anna. Mimi glares at me. It's getting late.

"Nobody could tell," Emily says. "I mean, how can you tell if someone's gay or not?"

Shawn shrugs. "I heard they smell different."

Emily rolls her eyes. She grabs his arm and steers him down the hall. I follow them, watching their feet and how they move forward one step at a time. Em snaps a picture of Shawn. He starts walking in such a happy way that it's almost like skipping. They are too cute.

Behind me someone hisses, "Fag hag."

I whirl around, but it's just blank faces, none of them stick in my head, they are all unfocused, except for their eyes. Their eyes stare.

But the truth is, I know all these eyes. There's Andrew. There's Mimi again. There's Aimee Ciciotte and Anna.

"Did you say something?" I ask Mimi. She shakes her head, but her mouth makes a tiny little smirk.

I do not give her the finger the way I want to, because I have class, damn it. Instead, I whirl back around and head into science.

"WE ARE GOING TO THE dance Friday," Emily announces as we examine our fetal pig's urinary system.

The pig's bladder looks suddenly, impossibly full. Oh, maybe that's my own.

"What?" I sit back in my chair, pull off my latex glove. My hand smells like a condom. I contemplate telling Emily about what someone, possibly Mimi, called me in the hall, but she looks so focused, it's not worth it.

"The dance. We're going," she says, not even looking at me, poking through the pig's innards.

I shake my head. "No way."

"Yep."

Emily invades the pig, works her way around like a pro, now that we've found its spleen. "This baby is ours," she said when we sat down. She took a picture of it. "No more girlie queasy crap. This baby is ours."

She pokes and prods. She careens through its insides. She explores and takes notes. I follow her lead, but wrongness fills my bones. We are invaders. We are defilers, slicing through muscles, moving protective sheaths to see what we will see.

"You have to get back out there," she says.

"No, I don't."

"Yes, you do," she slices something. "Damn. Hold this up."

Using this thin metal stick thing, I hold up a piece of abdominal muscle. She takes a picture of me and then goes back to work.

"Didn't you just say it was too soon for me to like somebody else?"

She slices deeper. "I changed my mind."

"I don't want to go," I tell her.

"You sound like a baby. 'I don't want to go.'" She peers into the pig's pelvic area. "No choice. Shawn and I will kidnap you."

"You're going with Shawn?"

She flashes smile glorious. "Mm-hhm."

"That's great!" I say and think, third wheel, third wheel.

Emily, the telepath, hears me somehow. "Like I've never been the third wheel."

"I didn't say that."

"You were thinking it," she sighs. "Do you think this is the ureter or the vagina?"

She giggles.

I shrug.

"We don't know the difference between a ureter and a vagina." She's dying now, laughing hysterically. She raises her hand and calls out, "Oh, Mr. Zeki! We can't tell the difference between the ureter and the vagina!"

Mr. Zeki struts over, hands on the hips of his too-tight chinos. "What are you? Junior girls or sophomore boys?"

Everybody cracks up. I drop the muscle. Emily snorts out her nose.

Mr. Zeki moves the muscle, uses the pointer, aims it at a tiny tube. "That, girls, is the ureter."

He winks. "You'll have to find your vagina on your own."

Red flames both our faces, but it's funny too. I hide my face in my hands and laugh and laugh until there is nothing left, until tears break through the surface of my eyes, until everything inside of me is gone, a dehydrated fetal pig without a soul.

EMILY AND I HAVE NEVER had a hard time getting guys, not since we passed that awkward stage in seventh grade where pudge made its home throughout my body and Emily resembled a mutated granola bar with braces and stringy hair.

She's a chocolate torte now. She's yummy with her super-model chestnut hair and her flirt eyes.

When you read "chick lit" you always find a hottie friend and a not hottie friend. One friend is always the ooh-la-la girl who everyone gravitates toward. The other is looked over, ignored, fading in the background while the other gallivants through French kissing hordes and muscle-man hands.

That's not how it ever was with us.

We always knew what guy would like which one of us. We'd split it up. Emily got artists, runners, metal heads, red-haired men, football players, Greek men. I'd get musicians, writers, Arab men, African-American men, soccer players. And gay men. Did I forget gay men? I did, didn't I?

Those lists are not all-inclusive of course. Shawn is a soccer player. One of my boyfriends freshman year was a runner. So, we mixed it up a bit.

"Everybody's got a type," Emily said once, after an Arab guy at the Bangor Mall ran after me, proposing.

I turned him down, blushing.

"They just like you 'cause you blush," she said. "It's so cute."

She made smooching noises at me. I socked her in the

arm and we went and bought shoes. She took pictures of our feet in every pair.

Now, I'm wondering, what if I don't have a type anymore? What if I go to this stupid dance thing and Shawn and Emily rip it up and I stand on the wall, staring at everyone else in couples, two by two going into the sex ark and I'm alone, alone, alone.

Or worse, what if my type is gay men trying not to be gay? What if the only guys who like me, like me as a last resort, the final shot at heterosexuality? What if I really am a beard? I'm obviously not a fag hag, but maybe I'm just someone people use for a disguise?

----o----

This is what I'm thinking when we pass Dylan in the hall. He's wearing a giant pink triangle on his black t-shirt, the universal symbol of gayness.

My breath whooshes out of me. My hand grabs Emily's arm.

Dylan waves at us and I walk up to him thinking, Breathe. Breathe.

"Dylan?"

He smiles at me and shrugs. "I figured it was time to just come out."

"You think that's a good idea?" Emily says. "Somebody's going to slam you."

"Dylan?" I say and in his name is all my worry and fear, rushing out of me like a broken guitar chord, like a sad, sad, song.

"I can handle myself." He just shrugs again. His green eyes burn into me. "People already know, anyway. How about you, Belle? You okay?"

"Yeah," I whisper.

He reaches out and touches my cheek, then drops his hand. "I know this is hard for you."

"No—it's . . ." My words flee. People walk by us. They turn their heads to stare.

"We're still friends, Belle," he says. "I still love you."

Emily throws up her hands. "Oh, Jesus! Give me a break."

She yanks me away, tearing me down the hall. "What is this, some kind of Danielle Steele novel?"

Behind us, someone calls Dylan a fag.

I can't tell who it was. Maybe it was everyone.

No, no, from the way he's glaring and the jutting of his chin, I think it was my neighbor, Eddie Caron. Or maybe, it was Colin Troust, that sophomore boy who lives up on Alton Ave. I don't know for sure. I don't know.

I glare at them both. They both glare back. Really. Eddie glares back. I shake my head. I do not know who anyone is anymore. And that's the problem. You spend all your life growing up in this hick place thinking you've got everyone all figured out. Anna is a jock and she'll be a real estate agent some day. Eddie is a neighbor boy, stupid but harmless, still hurting over what happened with Hannah. Dylan is my one true love, a hot, straight guy with golden hair and a bright smile.

Yep.

And what about me? What does Mr. Allen who runs the blueberry plant think about me? Or my mom's boss at the hospital, Mr. Jones? Or even my mom? Do they think, "There's Belle, she's got seizures but she's a damn good singer and she plays a fine guitar. Smart girl. She's got it together."

Is everyone as wrong about me as I am about them?

DYLAN? I THINK EDDIE CALLED you a fag, which is derived from the word faggot. Do you know what a faggot is? It's the bundle of wood they used to burn gay men with during medieval times. They'd burn people like you, Dylan. They said people like you were demons. Some people still say that. They're wrong, obviously. You're no demon.

They used to burn people with seizures too, said the demon got to them. They said that people with seizures were witches. Some people just call us freaks.

Go figure.

Maybe we were an appropriate couple after all. Five hundred years ago we'd have both died, not from the looks of people in the halls, but from the hands of people in our lives.

Burnt.

BEFORE EMILY AND I PART ways, me to German, her to PE, I grab her arm.

"I don't want him to get hurt," I tell her, my eyes watering.

She hugs me, my sister twin, my second body. She hugs me and murmurs, "I know."

I'M ALMOST IN THE DOOR to my German class when I hear someone mutter it.

"Fag hag."

I whip my head around, scan the kids moving speed-walker style past the tall, grey lockers. They've got books in their hands, not torches. Nobody's looking at me. They're all staring straight ahead, feet walking, mouths talking, eyes moving, hair in place. Good little soldiers, all.

Fag hag.

"Shut up," I say to all of them. "Shut up."

Nobody answers. They just goose-march ahead. One after the other after the other.

Then Anna says, "Did someone actually just call you fag hag?"

I scan the sophomores around me and whisper, "I think so."

Anna puts her hands on her soccer-goalie waist and says, "Whoever the hell just said that better shut the hell up."

I gasp. I've never heard Anna swear, not even when we lost Eastern Maines with a corner kick in the final three seconds her junior year.

She grabs me around the shoulders and says, "Freakin' idiot."

Then she kicks me in the shin and nods. "Stay tough, girl."

I nod. I'll stay tough.

WHAT A WEIRD DAY! BUT it isn't really. Because every day is crazy weird if you think of it. Every day some new person is born, some old person dies. Every day someone is loved for the first time and someone else is murdered for the only time.

I settle into my desk in German trying not to be pissed off about the fag hag comment. I mean, once is bad enough, but twice? I mean, what, I'm suddenly labeled? I'm not hurt-feelinged, I'm more sad. Plus, it was cool that Anna stood up for me like that.

Outside the window, the sky glows ski-parka blue and the trees sway in some frigid wind that I can't hear or feel. I should be out there with my arms outstretched. I should be out there rolling in the leaves, only I don't have anyone to roll with.

If sighing were acceptable I'd sigh right here but sighing, unfortunately, is a cliché.

Bob tiptoes in, without a pink triangle taped to his flannel shirt. He squints his eyes and looks at me through the corner of them. I wave. No hard feelings, I am trying to think. No hard feelings. Okay. A little hard feelings. He sits in his seat, looks around, starts scribbling a note to somebody. I bet it's Dylan.

Tom has seen them kiss. I will not imagine that.

In some weird, selfish way, I wish Dylan had cheated on me with a girl. That would make things easier. I could hate her. Emily and I could rant about what a tart she is, how she's bulimic or anorexic or should be (yes, that's awful). I could be mad, mad, mad and hate could be a tiger pushing me through the days. Plus, nobody would be muttering fag hag at me in the halls.

But, no. Gaydom soars through Dylan's Irish/Norwegian genes and his Gap jeans, probably. And I can't be mad, mad, mad because . . . well, he's oppressed. He's oppressed. He is no longer a dominant Aryan boy with his blonde hair and white skin and good parents and cute house. Now, he's a gay man. Now, he can be a victim.

I can't be angry about someone being gay, can I?

Poor Dylan. Poor Bob. Poor me.

That's the only time I'm going to say that. Okay. One more time. Poor me.

That's actually fun to say. I am such a Mallory.

----o----

"How you doing, Commie?" Tom says when he sits down.

I don't even look at him. "You don't have to be nice to me."

"What?"

I yank a notebook out of my backpack even though we never take notes in here. "I said, 'You don't have to be nice to me just because your dad told you to.'"

His breath blows out his mouth and hits hot against my neck. I pull at my ponytail and try to fix it but I do not turn around.

"Is that what you think?" His voice comes out as scorching as his breath.

I shrug.

"That's stupid."

I shrug again, which is not the best comeback. My palms tingle. I pull out my ponytail holder and start all over again.

"That's not it at all."

"What is it then?" I say.

He is silent. Then he says, "God, you really don't know?"

----o----

Herr Reitz passes back our tests from yesterday. I'm afraid to turn mine over.

Tom taps me on the back. That's what he does when he wants to share. I breathe in deep, afraid to look at him, afraid of what I'll see in his eyes. I turn and see them, tree-bark brown and strong. There's no pity there. No lies.

I hold my test up. Ninety-eight. Two points off for forgetting an umlaut. *Love, love me do . . .*

Tom holds his up. One hundred.

Bob's all alone. Not even Rasheesh is asking him what he got. Sorry, I should call him Crash. That's what Rasheesh has renamed himself.

"Bob," I say, while Herr Reitz starts opening windows to let October leaf air in. "How'd you do?"

Deer caught in the headlights, he stares and stares at me.

"What?" he croaks it out.

"You do okay?" I ask him. I turn sideways to face him, look over at Tom, he's got a dog-eating-peanut-butter grin on his face, but Bob, Bob gives me a real smile and holds up his test.

"Ninety-seven."

"Excellent," I say. He keeps smiling. Tom shakes his head and once Herr Reitz starts talking a little folded-up note flips over my shoulder and lands on my notebook. I bite my lip and unfold it.

I should start calling you, Softie.

I snort.

I write back: *You better not.*

I toss it over my shoulder when Herr Reitz starts the radio. We're singing again. "All You Need is Love" this time.

"All together now!" Herr Reitz shouts. He's dressed in green scrubs today. He lifts up his mask to sing.

The note flips back to me.

You like Commie better, it says.

I scribble and sing, scribble and sing. Herr Reitz shouts, "Louder."

I write: *I like Belle best.*

Tom gets the note, scribbles again in his boy writing, straight, scrawling yet tight.

I unfold the note: *Softie fits you better.*

When Herr Reitz turns around and starts dancing, I discreetly salute Tom with my finger. He laughs and laughs and laughs. Even Herr Reitz notices.

"Want to share, Tom?" he asks.

Tom lifts up his hands like he's about to be hit by a speeding car. "No . . . No. That's okay."

The moment Herr Reitz isn't looking, the note flips back.

Didn't know you had it in you . . . Softie Commie Belle Pinko.

I write back: *Thanks. What's your name again? Is it Tom, Dick, or Hairy?*

Tom chortles again and I smile too. And then I realize it, for the first time in years, I'm not thinking about Dylan. I'm not thinking about Dylan at all, and the greatest part of this is that I don't feel bad about that. I don't feel bad at all.

He shoots me one more note, this time it's on a piece of duct tape folded up and stuck together. The duct tape is shaped like a tiny soccer ball, but it's still a note because there's writing on it.

It's a quote.

Of course.

I have to twirl the ball around to read it all. The letters are miniscule, just absolutely tiny.

It says: Embrace your desires. They make us love, make us create, make us long, make us live.

Hhmm. I don't know how to kick that ball back to him, or even if I want to.

Reasons Why Calling Me a Fag Hag Is Not Cool

1. Because it's bigoted. Duh.

2. Because it is not the most clever of rhymes.

3. It's not appropriate. I'm really a beard.

4. Because all fag hag means is that I don't care if a guy is gay and that I'm still friends with him.

5. Which I don't know if it's really true. If I am friends with him. I want to be, but he lied to me.

6. Because it makes me sound like I have long, stringy, tangled hair and a wart on my nose, which I most emphatically do not and if I did then I would have it removed. Nor do I cackle.

7. Because if you do it again, whoever you are, I will pound your face into the locker until it is unrecognizable and people looking at your yearbook photo will shirk away, afraid, very afraid. Well, I would if I weren't a pacifist. I will, however, most certainly think about doing this.

AFTER FAR TOO MANY GERMAN Beatles songs, Herr Reitz turns off the stereo and beams at us. He reaches around his back to tie his scrubs tighter.

"So, are we all psyched to go to the German restaurant tomorrow?"

Crash groans. I slam my head with my hand.

"Belle, liebchen, did you forget?" Herr Reitz asks.

I nod and blush.

We are going to some German restaurant in Bangor tomorrow. Meeting after school. People are driving their own cars or riding with Herr Reitz. I cannot ride with Herr Reitz and I cannot drive. Damn seizures. Why didn't Emily take German?

Tom leans over and mumbles, "Drive with me, okay? I don't want to get stuck with Crash or Bob."

I turn around. His eyes don't show signs of teasing. His hair sticks up a little in back. His fingers are fiddling with some duct tape, making something. "Yeah?"

"Yeah."

I squint my eyes, point my finger, try to be a hardie not a softie. "No name calling."

He makes a fake frown. "Not even Softie?"

I make my hand a fist. He grabs it in his much bigger hand. His fingers curl around my hand. I shiver. He holds onto it for a second and then lets go.

Crash giggles like he's two years old or something. "Some-body likes Bel-le."

Tom blows him off and says, "What are you, like six?"

Crash laughs and skips out of the room, more like he's four. Tom shakes his head, watches him go, and hands the duct tape he's been working on to me. His fingertips graze the palm of my hand.

"It's a guitar," he says.

It is. It's a perfect tiny guitar, with twisted-up duct tape for the strings and a hole in the center.

"Wow," I say. "I can keep this?"

He nods, stands up, and rocks a little bit on the balls of his feet. Herr Reitz scoots by and yells, "No hanky panky in here, guys."

I glare at my teacher. My teacher laughs.

"It's really good. It's like a sculpture," I say to Tom once Herr Reitz is completely out the door. "You're really into duct tape."

"I'm really into a lot of things," Tom grabs his books and I blush hot and crazy and shove that comment right out of my mind and then he says, "You sure you don't need a ride home?"

"Yeah."

When he leaves, I sit there and sit there, staring at my little duct tape guitar and wonder why my hand tingles like this, like electricity, like love meter and passion twist and good, good things.

I am not so shallow that I'm over my one true love already. I am not. I refuse to be.

I grab my things and follow everyone else out the

door. Still tingling, my hand wraps itself around the duct tape guitar.

- - - - o - - - -

Emily and I trot through the old pale halls. It smells like sloppy Joes and sneakers. Just a few stragglers, overachievers like us, hustle off to soccer or cross-country practice, heading to clubs. It's like the paleness of the halls has swallowed everybody up, pinned them into lockers or paled them out of existence. Maybe the dullness of it pushed them out the school doors, into their cars, the yellow rinky-dink busses, the sidewalk toward home and work and home and work.

"There's not much to look forward to in life, is there?" I ask Emily.

"The dance," she says.

I groan.

She tries again, because Emily is like that, an Energizer Bunny–type friend, but instead of keep going and going, she keeps trying and trying. "Freeing the oppressed? Stopping the torture? Ending human rights violations?"

We have Amnesty International after school today. I'm the president. My mom's big into Amnesty because she founded it back when she was in high school. Then it was all about apartheid (my mom calls it apart-hate) in South Africa and El Salvador. Now, it's about genocide, torturing suspected terrorists, and women's rights. It's crazy that twenty-five years have passed and we're still fighting over the same things: respecting people, recognizing that people are people, human kindness.

My hands tremble and the Postum I guzzled down at lunch sloshes in my otherwise empty stomach.

Emily grabs my elbow. "You okay?"

I nod. I think about the little duct tape guitar I put in my purse. "Yep. I'm good. No. I'm scared."

"It's okay to be scared," she says.

"I'm a weenie."

"You're not a weenie."

"You don't think so?"

She laughs. "No, just a dweeb."

Dylan is in Amnesty International . . . I'm afraid to see him . . . I have to see him.

Em whips out her camera.

I put my hands up, pleading. "Not another picture."

"No," she flips it around so I can see the back where you review the pictures. "Look at this."

It's a picture of me, way too close. "Ew. You can see my pores."

She pokes me in the arm. "No you can't. Look at the whole picture."

My face is white, my eyes are down and seem about to tear. Everything about this girl is drooping.

"Is this the picture you took at my house after Dylan dumped me?" I ask her, pushing the camera away. Em keeps her "important" pictures on her camera. She can store about 150 on there. She downloads most of them, but the ones she wants to remind herself about she keeps, so she can just stare at them any time. I do not like that this is one of those "important" pictures. My body heavies thinking about how sad I look.

"No," she shuts the camera off. "It's what you looked like right after you were named Harvest Queen and Dylan kissed you and then went over to high-five Bob."

I swallow. She waits. I swallow again. "You think I've always known somehow?"

She shrugs. She hugs me. She says, "I think the two of you were not meant to be."

THERE'S A PART OF ME that does not want to think that I always knew something was wrong. There's a part of me that wants to shake my head and stomp my feet and make it all go away. This is probably the same part that didn't look at the evidence that was right before my eyes, and even though I know this, it doesn't stop me from defending the fairy tale.

Words tumble out of me, "But he was so perfect. He was the best hugger ever and he was so philosophical."

"Preachy."

I glare at her. "Philosophical."

Em grabs her camera again and fiddles with it. I wait. I try to breathe slowly, good, deep breaths. Finally she says, "Do you ever think that maybe you romanticize Dylan a little bit? You know, you only think about his good stuff and forget how he always burped after he ate spaghetti or how much his feet stank and stuff."

"I don't do that," I say, but even as I say it the truth of it sinks into my stomach and pits itself there. I ignore it and grab Em's hand, yanking her toward our meeting. "We're so late."

We bullet into the classroom, the president and the vice president.

"Late as usual," announces Julie Speyer, but she's smiling. People are used to Emily and me being late.

"Sorry." I blush and look around.

There's no golden blonde boys. There's no newly announced gay boys with pink triangles on their shirts and sparkles in their green, green eyes. My breath escapes my mouth, pushed out by tongue and tension. I imagine it's wind that whips across the classroom, touching the walls, looking for him everywhere. He's not here, it tells me. Not here.

I breathe back in, maybe relieved, maybe disappointed, maybe both. I tell my hands to stop trembling and start the meeting.

I can do this. I can live my life. I can.

I read them this, taken directly off the Amnesty website. By the time I get to the end I can hear the tension in my voice rising.

Amnesty International today welcomed the detention of former Peruvian President Alberto Fujimori and called upon Chile to ensure that he stays in the country pending a judicial determination whether to extradite him to Peru or to try him in Chile.

Amnesty International considers that the widespread and systematic nature of the human rights violations that were committed under the government of Alberto Fujimori between 1990 and 2000 constitute crimes against humanity under international law. During his term in office, Amnesty International documented hundreds of cases of "disappearances" and extrajudicial executions. In addition, torture and ill-treatment by the Peruvian security forces throughout the ten years that Alberto Fujimori was in power were widespread.

How can things in the world get to be so wrong?

"That sucks!" Kara Raymond of the black clothes and multiple piercings shouts. Back in grade school, she used to wear all purple and looked like Barney, the annoying dinosaur on PBS, that's because she's built like Barney, with too much in the front. She doesn't have a green belly or a tail though.

"Let's write letters," Emily says.

Kara pumps her fist in the air. Her bracelets jangle. "Letters!"

I clear my throat. "Can I read the next one?"

Everyone nods for me to go ahead. I clear my throat. This one goes for the gusto, because this one is about us.

I read and as I do the door pops open and Dylan, golden boy, all serious comes in. He shoves his hands in his pockets. The edges of his pink triangle crumple and curl in, as if they're rebelling and attempting to become a parallelogram or a trapezoid, something, anything other than a triangle.

MUHAMMAD FARAJ AHMED BASHMILAH AND SALAH NASSER SALIM 'ALI

THESE TWO FRIENDS FROM YEMEN TOLD AMNESTY INTERNATIONAL THAT THEY WERE ARRESTED, DETAINED, AND TORTURED FOR SEVERAL DAYS IN JORDAN. THEY SAID THAT THEY WERE THEN HELD INCOMMUNICADO WITHOUT CHARGE OR TRIAL IN UNKNOWN LOCATIONS FOR MORE THAN A YEAR AND A HALF. THEY SAID THEY WERE TRANSPORTED BETWEEN DETEN-

Emily's hand shoots up to cover her mouth. She stares at me. I stare at her.

Julie Speyer sputters in her chair, but Kara's lost all her manic energy, depressed, overwhelmed.

"It's like El Salvador all over again," I say. "Only we are the ones who make people disappear."

My words seem hollow to me, just hollow. I don't know why I think we can do anything, ever. We can't even fix ourselves. One of the millions of long fluorescent lights in the room sputters above my head.

"We've got to do something," Emily says, scratching at some dry skin on her hand. "More letters?"

No one says anything. The light blanks out, but the others stay on so no one notices.

"I'm sick of writing letters," I sit up straight. I put down my papers. "How about a concert?"

"A concert."

"Yeah, like a benefit concert," I say. "A benefit for the disappeared. We could have local groups play."

"That's cool," Julie says. "And the next night we could do like a poetry reading or something. And the next night something else."

"Yeah, a whole week of stuff," Brian, the quiet boy in the back says.

We all tuck our hair behind our ears, except Kara. She's

shaved hers off. We all get started. We all know it might not do anything, nobody might pay attention.

"But we've got to try," I mutter. "We've got to try."

"Don't you think," Dylan says, "that maybe we should start working on discrimination at home, instead of overseas?"

No one says anything.

He stomps all the way into the room, swings the door shut behind him. Emily's breath whizzes out between her teeth. My hands shake. I swallow. I remember to breathe in, breathe out, breathe in.

Beautiful Dylan boy looks at all of us, one at a time. He is on fire, his gold glow is fire glow and it rages around us unstoppable. "Do you know how many people called me a fag today?"

No one answers.

He hits the wall with his fist and we all jump. We're a pretty pacifist group, Amnesty International. We aren't used to violence in our actual presence and Dylan is a strong guy.

"Thirty-seven!" he shouts at us. "Thirty-seven people called me a fag. I thought these people were my friends. I can list them! Belle, you want me to list them? Dakota Murphy, Jake Star, Mimi Cote, Eddie Caron, Colin Troost . . ."

All his gold anger ebbs away as we watch him crumple. Julie stands and opens up her arms. Dylan steps into them and she hugs him. He leans into her body. That should be my body, supporting him, keeping him up. Soon, one by one, all the members of Amnesty International walk over to Dylan and Julie and hug them. Arms wrap around backs. Shoulders and bellies press together. Heads bow.

I sit on the top of the desk and watch them. Emily comes over and grabs my hand. Without saying anything, she pulls me over to the group and we reach out our arms and try to encircle them, but we can't, we can't. The bodies are too many. The need is too big.

"Postum was created by Charles Post. He went to this town in Michigan for a health cure and decided that coffee and caffeine were the root of all evils. So, he created Postum and the Postum Cereal Company. He started Postum and then he created Grape Nuts," I tell Emily in the car on the way home. We have not talked about the meeting. We have not talked about Dylan.

"Fascinating," Emily pops some gum in her mouth, presses hard on the gas. "We're stopping at Shawn's house."

"What?" I slam my feet up on her dashboard and admire my Snoopy shoes, which feature a lovely image of Snoopy on the top. Snoopy is smiling and holding balloons. I got them back in eighth grade when my uncle went to Spain. They are canvas and comfortable and they have a hole in the toe, which makes them look a little ratty to discerning shoe connoisseurs, but I don't care. They are my favorite shoes in the world but Dylan has always hated them. I have decided to start wearing them again. "Why are we stopping at Shawn's?"

"He asked."

"I have homework," I say. Emily wiggles her eyebrows at me, because she knows I don't have much. We have almost all the same classes. Sighing, I ask, "Is soccer practice done?"

"Yep."

We drive in silence for a second and she says, "Do you think he's cute?"

"Yeah," I make my feet dance in front of me, a happy little dance. I think about my little duct tape guitar safely stashed in my person. "I think Shawn is cute."

But it's not really Shawn I'm thinking about.

She sighs and smiles, sighs and smiles and I imagine little red-crayon hearts floating above her head. "I think he's really cute."

"Uh-huh," I say. "Did you know that Charles Post gave his business to his daughter when she turned twenty-seven? She was one of the first businesswomen in America. How cool is that?"

She turns off the stereo, parks in a driveway outside a little ranch house that I assume must belong to Shawn's parents. It's nestled in some blueberry fields. The wind whips a piece of a blueberry bush across the driveway. "You know, I can try not to like him or talk about it. Is it bugging you that I like somebody, cause I know you're a little vulnerable right now."

"I'm not vulnerable," I slam my Snoopy shoes down off the dashboard. The broken-up blueberry bush blows against the house like tumbleweed. I make my voice sound Russian. "I am strong, strong woman, hear me roar."

My door zips open and Tom is smiling there. He calls to Shawn across the driveway. "See? I told you she was a pinko."

Snoopy hides behind his doghouse, but I take Tom's hand and leave the car. One foot. Another. I go on.

----o----

In Shawn's house, we all chomp on frozen burritos, microwaved of course, and settle into old couches in Shawn's basement. Shawn's basement is half-remodeled.

There's walls and flooring, but the ceiling is pipes and electrical wires. There's a big TV facing the couches and in another corner is a mess of work-out equipment.

Em and Shawn snuggle close to each other on this incredibly ugly plaid couch, so close that their thighs touch and I can imagine how Em's leg feels, warm and super charged.

Me?

Tom and I are on the other couch, not too close, not too far. I can see the new quote he's written on the duct tape strip on his shoe: I like getting hit in the head by the ball.

So he did put on a soccer quote. I smile.

We've done all the college talk about where everyone's applied and we've got some overlaps. Everyone but Em's applying to Bates, which is a pretty good school, all top-twenty liberal arts college and all that. She pouts and sticks her tongue out and then says, "I'm just an individual, that's all."

"You can say that again," Shawn teases. She hits him.

"Want to go get a Coke?" he says.

She leaps up. "Yep."

"You guys?" Shawn nods at us.

"No thanks," I say. Coke has caffeine. I miss caffeine.

Tom shakes his head and when they're gone he turns his body to face me. "You doing okay?"

"Yeah."

"Anna told me someone called you a fag hag in the hall today."

I shrug. "No big. You don't need to protect me, you know."

His hands, his calf muscles pushing against the upholstery. Some big. I turn away. I will not think about him that way. It's too soon.

He leans down, unzips his backpack, and pulls out some duct tape. He rips off two chunks and gives me one. It's sticky and gray and shiny. I hold it far away from me. "What am I supposed to do with this?"

He's already twisting his up, making arms, legs, a little man, maybe? "Play with it. Make something. It calms me down when I'm spazzing."

"I am not spazzing."

I try to twist the tape. It sticks to my fingers. I'm hopeless. I look up into Tom's tree-bark eyes. I breathe in the scent of him, spicy and clean, against the faint wet smell of the basement.

I say, whisper light, "Do you need that? To calm down?"

He nods, looks me straight on, and says, "When I'm with you, I do."

My lips press together and my heart wiggles in my chest, which it should not be doing because I am in mourning over my past relationship. And if my heart is already wiggling that must mean that my past relationship is not what I thought it was. I shake my head.

"Really?" I manage to say and then regret it.

"Really." His eyes are so brown.

We stare at each other. Upstairs Em and Shawn thump around. We keep staring. A slow smile creeps across Tom's face and he reaches across the couch and takes my hand in his. It feels like every single nerve ending in my body is about to explode. I loved Dylan, I know I loved Dylan, but it never felt crazy like this, like fire and cold and lyrics floating across my skin. I gulp and Tom runs his thumb across my hand.

"Do you ever think about what might have happened if Mimi hadn't asked me out in eighth grade?" he asks, his voice all husky and low.

I gulp. I look away at the stairs. Shawn and Em are nowhere to be found. I can't help it. It's like he's a magnet. I look back at Tom and my voice answers for me, "Sometimes."

"Me too," he says.

"But *I* ended up with the *gay* guy," I say trying to pass it off lightly, like it's a happy thing. "While Mimi ended up with the soccer stud."

"Yep," Tom squeezes my hand and looks at me hard, like he's trying to see inside me. I squirm and sit up straighter but don't pull away my hand.

Then I do what I do when I'm uncomfortable. I babble.

"Do you ever think that our lives are like folk songs? You know. Or maybe Bruce Springsteen songs. I know he's rock, but he's such a good writer he seems like folk, especially his ancient stuff. You know, like we're all trying to get out of the Valley, like in that Gorka song, or we're born to run like that Springsteen song. But it's like I'm stuck in the wrong song. I want to be in a Dar Williams song where I see the beauty of the rain, which is a song of hers, or a Christine Lavin song because she's so crazy and funny and quirky and happy, but it's like I'm stuck in this song of longing and want, you know and have you ever even heard of Dar Williams or Bruce—"

Tom does it then. He just leans in really smooth and I guess he's been getting closer the whole time I've talked because all of a sudden his other hand is on the side of my face. His lips press against my lips, soft and good but really, really there and it's a good thing I'm sitting down because if I wasn't sitting down I would absolutely, positively fall down because I am stereotypically weak in the knees.

Yikes.

I am kissing someone other than Dylan. Something sparkles behind my eyelids. I open my eyes back up and see Tom's long eyelashes, the darkness of his skin.

I pull away and jump up, turn around, sit back down, put my face in my hands, shake my head.

"Belle?" Tom's voice echoes against my ears. "I'm sorry. I thought you—"

"No!" I say, awkward, my heart thumping, my neurons firing. "No, it's okay. It was just—I wasn't expecting it or anything."

I take a peek at him. That muscle in his cheek twitches and his face is definitely a deeper color like maybe he's blushing. He looks scared. I've never seen him look this scared, not when taking a penalty kick, not even when giving those German oral reports.

"I mean," I rush out and grab his hand. "I really liked it. I like it a lot. I liked it way too much."

I am an idiot.

He smiles at me and his scared eyes turn happy again. "I liked it too, Commie."

I pull my hand out of his and cross my arms in front of my chest. "I am not a commie."

He starts to say something back, but Em and Shawn tromp back down the stairs, Em grabs me by the hand, all panicky looking. "We have to go, now. I completely forgot I have a dentist's appointment."

"But?" I say, yanked up off my happy couch place with Tom, a delicious-looking happy couch boy. No, he isn't. Yes, he is. "But . . ."

I know Em just had her dentist's appointment last Thursday and I know she had no cavities. She is always proud about the fact she's never had a cavity.

She glares at me and I get it. She's lying.

"Oh, right. Yeah, I forgot too," I say and we wave bye and scramble up the stairs, still holding hands, Em still pulling me along.

She slams into her car and says, "I got my thing."

"Oh!" I say and start laughing.

"It. Is. Not. Funny," she accentuates every word. She hates her thing, she hates buying tampons. She'd like to pretend she's still ten, I guess. "I have no tampons."

"Oh," I say, straightening up, but the horrified look on her face just makes me laugh more.

"You have to come with me to buy some," she says, turning on the car, shifting into reverse, and hightailing it out of Shawn's driveway. The car squeals.

I shake my head. "Emily, you are a big girl. I think it's time you faced your fears."

She shifts into forward and heads down the road. "You have to come with me."

"Dolly is not going to think any less of you if you buy tampons. People buy condoms there, remember?" I try not to laugh and put my Snoopy shoes up on the dashboard.

"Dolly thinks I'm eight."

"You act like you're eight," I laugh and smile.

Dolly runs the local Rite Aid. She's only about 115 years old, with no teeth, sweet eyes, and smoker's voice. She knows everybody and everything in town, and she tells you all about it.

"You don't have any at home?" I ask Em as she whizzes the car past the Y and Harmon's Auto Tire. She cuts off Ray Davis's black pickup truck and speeds through a yellow light, one of our town's four stoplights.

"I'm sure! Would I have ditched Shawn if I didn't have to?" she yells, slamming into a stop at our town's second of four stoplights.

I put my hands up in surrender. "Okay. Okay. I will go in with you and I will buy them for you but you have to stand with me when I buy them."

She smiles and relaxes, she turns on WERV, the alternative community radio station I love but she hates. "Deal."

I wait until the light turns green and then I say it, "Tom kissed me."

"What!" She swerves, hits the divider, and bounces back into the lane again. "He did what?"

I shrug and smile and Em shakes her head and laughs, and laughs. Then she says all triumphantly, "Well, I guess we are definitely going to that dance and you are definitely no Mallory."

"What do you mean?"

"Well, you're obviously not sulking anymore, moaning, whining, crying, sobbing, gesticulating, grousing, complaining, brooding, acting all morose . . ."

I make a pout face and she laughs harder. "Shut up. I think I'm rebounding."

"So?"

"Well, that's no good," I pull up my Snoopy sneaker and start fiddling with the laces.

"Why not?"

"Then it's not real," I say. Anna drives by and waves. We wave back.

Em gives a happy little toot and says, "I love Anna." Then she turns back to the conversation, "Nothing is ever real, Belle."

She keeps driving with one hand and swerving and taking pictures out the window and I think about all the ways I felt with Dylan. I think about the me I was with Dylan, singing show tunes instead of folk, never using parmesan cheese on my spaghetti because he hated the way it smelled, watching old sci-fi movies even when I hated them, making myself like them anyway because that's what Dylan wanted me to be.

My heart hits my throat. I am lost without Dylan but I lost myself with Dylan. I am a cliché. "Nothing's ever real really," I say. "Nobody's ever who we think they are."

"Emotions are real," Em says, turning on her blinker at the light. I give her the thumbs-up sign for remembering. "Emotions are real just not the reasons behind them. Feelings are real, you just never really know that what you're basing them on is real."

The light turns green. Em takes a wickedly wide left turn. I mock her. "Happy advice, oh sage one."

She bops me in the arm. "Shut up."

I do. I wait until she's turned into Rite Aid and pulled into a spot, but still I don't speak. She puts the car in park, turns to me, and says, "What do you feel when you're with Tom?"

I grimace at the stupid touchy-feely aspect of this question but answer anyways. "Lots of stuff. Confused. Scared. Happy. Safe."

Em smiles. "See? That's too complicated to be fake."

"Yeah."

"And when he kissed you, how did you feel?"

I close my eyes, but I don't have to do that to remember it. Just thinking about that kiss makes my heart a happy thump-thump song. "Giddy. I felt giddy. Shut up."

She laughs and then panic hits me and I grab Em's arm. "What if he's gay, too? What if only gay men like me because I'm not threatening or something?"

"That's stupid," Em pulls her keys out of the ignition and pockets them.

"No, it's not."

"Belle, I don't think Tom Tanner is gay."

"But what if he is? What if every man is? What if no one is ever who we think they are?

"Well, what do you think? That it's all polarities? Like all gay or all straight all the time?" Em unbuckles her seat belt, shifts forward in the seat, grabs the steering wheel like she's still driving. "Maybe it's all shades and everybody is a little bit gay or a lot bit gay or no gay or they shift around. I don't know."

I point at her. "You have been watching too many self-help shows again."

"Shut up. I don't know. It's just a theory."

"So according to your theory, you are a little bit gay," I wiggle my eyebrows at her to show her how ridiculous this is.

"Well, I mean, you're looking kind of cute with those bacon lips," she laughs.

I stick my tongue out at her. "You are so not gay."

She crosses her arms in front of her chest. "It doesn't make my theory wrong."

"This isn't about your theory. It's about me. It's about whether or not I'm some sort of fag hag."

"That's a stupid name. Hanging around with gay men is not a big deal," she sighs and shifts her weight in the seat again, looking uncomfortable. "You seriously think Tom is gay?"

"No, but I didn't think Dylan was gay either." I shove my hair into a ponytail, which is what I sometimes do when I'm serious about things. "I feel like I don't know who anyone is."

Em's eyes grip mine. I stop fidgeting with my hair. "You know who you are, right?"

Everything in me heavies. I unbuckle my seatbelt, like I'm going to free myself from the truth somehow, but the truth tumbles out my mouth anyways.

"No," I shake my head. "I don't."

Em grabs her camera, fiddles with a button, and shows me an old picture of me. Freshman year. Singing in the talent show with Gabriel against my chest. My eyes smile. My fingers strum an old John Gorka tune, a silly one about Saint Caffeine.

Her eyes glint with something fierce and determined and she flicks off the monitor. "You are Belle Philbrick. You are a fantastic folk singer, a good student, my best friend, a sweet political activist who can't drink coffee, and you are my best friend. Did I already say that?"

I nod, bite my lip, and she grabs me by the shoulders and says, "And you are also going to buy me some freaking tampons before things get really ugly."

I jump back and the urge for crying passes. "Oh, I'm so sorry. I completely forgot."

She puts her camera in her pocket and opens the door. "Yeah. But I didn't."

----o----

We sneak through the front door of Rite Aid like cat burglars. We walk in sideways, looking over our shoulders.

"Doorway clear," I say to Em in my best military voice, which even I have to admit, isn't all that good.

She pulls her hair over her face to hide it. She makes her fingers like a pretend gun, unholstered and ready at her side. "Check. I'll survey the perimeter."

She sashays away before I can yell at her, the sneak. She's just checking out the perimeter so that she doesn't have to go down the tampon aisle. Wimp. She didn't even bring her camera in here. Double wimp.

I shake my head, pull my hair out of my coat collar, and walk past Dolly, who flips through a tabloid at the register wearing her cute little blue apron.

"Why Belle Philbrick!" she says with a big smile. "Isn't it good to see you here, little missy. How's the singing?"

"Good," I say, smiling back at Dolly and her gums.

She leans her tiny, old body across the counter. "Any record deals, yet?"

I laugh. "Hardly."

She slaps the counter with her hand, which has only 800,000 rings on it. "You be patient. You'll be a superstar, mark my words."

I don't have the heart to tell Dolly that I don't want to be a superstar so I just smile and nod, which is my good-girl reaction to situations of this sort. Dolly stands back up straight. "How's your mumma? Still singing the wrong words?"

Everyone in town knows about my mother's wrong-words syndrome. According to Dolly, my mom was kicked out of the high school's show choir because of it. I'm not supposed to ask about that though because Dolly said it might "hit too close to the bone."

"She's good," I say and cast a glance over my shoulder for Em. She's obviously still scoping out the perimeter. She will probably scope out the perimeter until I've completed the transaction, she's such a wimp.

Dolly makes her voice one decibel quieter than a jet landing in Bangor. "What'cha here for, honey?"

I step up to the counter and make my voice a whisper. "Girl things."

Dolly leans forward so I can smell the cigarettes on her clothes. Her eyes twinkle behind her glasses. "You stuck buying tampons for Emily again?"

I straighten up, shocked. My hand zips over my mouth.

Dolly slaps her hip with her hand and hee-haws. "Like she thinks I don't know. That's one uptight chicken."

I giggle. Dolly winks and I walk down the feminine-products aisle. She calls after me and I turn around and she mouths a word, but I'm not sure what it is. Maybe "Dylan?" I wish I could read lips. I give her a little wave and turn away. My Snoopy shoes slide on the smooth linoleum and take me past the douches and sanitary pads, the weird medicine stuff for yeast infections to the nice blue and white boxes of the tampon section.

I look for slender regular. How ridiculous it is that I know what kind of tampon Emily uses. I decide I deserve the BEST FRIEND OF THE YEAR AWARD.

"That girl owes me," I say.

That's when I hear it, the low, deep laugh of Dylan when he's trying not to laugh. It's a snort really. That always happens when he's trying really hard not to guffaw, like the time one of Em's tampons fell out of her locker and she had to stomp on it with her foot to hide it.

Dylan's here. My breath catches in my chest. I should try to warn him again, about what Tom's dad said, I think, or tell him that I'm so sorry he had to lie to be with me. I grab a tampon box and walk around to his aisle.

It takes me a second to figure out what it is I'm seeing under Rite Aid's fluorescent lights. It's Dylan and he's struggling so hard not to laugh that he's leaning into the guy next to him. The guy next to him has his arm around Dylan's shoulders and it looks as if he's smelling Dylan's hair. It's Bob. Of course, it's Bob.

My heart falls to the floor. They look so happy, even Bob. He's smiling and chuckling and Dylan's golden glow seems to have touched him too.

I reach out and grab a shelf to steady myself.

Dylan has flown away from me. How far away love goes. A tiny part of my heart is so happy to see him safe and laughing, but the other part is a black pit that threatens to suck all of me into it. He is happy without me. He is laughing without me. But what about me? I kissed Tom.

Okay, I will be above this, I think and I start walking down the aisle. One step. Another. Bob sees me first and his smile vanishes just like that. My hand zooms up and checks my hair. Bob nudges Dylan in the ribs and he looks up too. The happy vanishes from his eyes in less than a second and he looks down into his hand. I look there too. He clutches an industrial-size variety package of condoms. His eyes glance up at Bob. Bob's face turns bright red.

I swallow. Condom purchases are a whole different league than kissing on the couch.

My Snoopy shoes stop walking.

Dylan's face doesn't move. His body doesn't move. His eyes are just sad, sad, sad guitar strings with no one to play them. No, that's me.

Bob is the one whose mouth moves. "Belle."

He says my name like an apology.

He says my name like a bad dream.

He says my name like it's the end of the world.

I swallow. I tilt my head. Em's feet stride down the aisle behind me. I make myself say the words with a kind smile. "Well, at least you're practicing safe sex."

No one says anything and Em finally makes it to my side. She gasps.

"Oh my God," she says. It would be a hiss but there are no "s" sounds. It's more like a snarl. She turns into her angry teenage girl mode, hands on her hips, face flushed. "I am all for protection and I am all for being gay and able to express your love in any anal-orifice way possible, but could you have not waited like a week or something?"

She looks like an angry mother. Her mouth twitches. Her eyes squint to half their size and her head bebops around with her words. Her right hand points at the boys, an accusation. Bob backs up and bumps into Dylan. Dylan puts himself in front of Bob, protecting him.

"We can do whatever we want to, Emily," he says. His voice is strong and sure. This is Dylan at his toughest. I used to call him "Viking" when he got like this, like the time he was so upset that Mr. Patrick gave me a ninety on my Plath essay. This is the Dylan I remember, not someone about to kill himself or go hide, but a man who knows what he wants and what's right. A little part of me is so proud of him.

Emily takes a deep breath, brings her hands down to her hips again. "I know you can, but think about Belle. She loved you. Have a little respect."

I glare at her and find my voice. "Emily!"

She shakes her head, snatches the tampon box from me, and walks away.

Dylan steps back to Bob's side, grabs for his hand but only manages to clasp his wrist, and looks at me, all his anger melted away. "I still love you, Belle. Just not that way."

I walk past them, everything inside of me churning and mixed up. There's all this anger and guilt and there's no words to describe it, even if I had Gabriel, I don't think I could make the right music to express it. It would take an orchestra.

So I walk past them, mouth closed. There is nothing I can say.

AFTER I GET ALL MY homework done, I shrug on my jacket and stand in our front yard, leaning against a tree, staring up at the sky.

I remember. It was about a month ago and Dylan had just given some concert in Augusta. Everyone crowded around him afterwards, even though he was part of a choral ensemble. He'd had an important solo. People stood around him, basking in his glow, like he was some sort of superstar. He smiled at each of them, talked to everyone, wasn't flip, wasn't cocky, was humble and good.

I waited near the back of the church where they'd be singing, hanging out with Em near the table that held the extra hymnals, letting Dylan get all the praise he deserved. He caught my eye and winked. Then Bob pushed his way through the crowd and hugged him, really tightly. Dylan hugged him back.

I turned to Em. "Let's go wait outside."

There's something about the outside that is so much better than the in.

I know that some people know they are gay all their lives. I know that some people sort of know but they fight it. I know that some people never admit it to themselves and no matter how much it hurts thinking about Dylan loving Bob, I know it's better that he knows, that he allows himself to be who he is. No matter how hard that is.

And who am I?

I am Belle Philbrick, kisser of Tom Tanner, player of guitar, friend of Emily.

I sigh, roll myself around on my toes so that my head touches the bark of a maple tree. The bark roughs my skin. The cold air pushes through my clothes.

Someone coughs. I whirl around and see Eddie.

He walks toward me, hands in his pockets. "You okay, Belle?"

"Yeah," I laugh, embarrassed, "just telepathically communicating to the trees."

He stands there staring at me, not sure what to make of me, I guess. He doesn't have a coat on. His eyes tighten. "Why'd you do it, Belle?"

"Do what?" A light turns on at Mrs. Darrow's.

He chokes out a laugh. "Go out with him."

I place my hand flat against the bark of the tree. "I loved him."

Now Eddie does laugh. "He's a fag."

"That's crap, Eddie. That's a crappy thing to say." I let go of the tree, stand up straight. Something small moves in the woods behind me, but I don't turn around.

"But he is. He's a faggot."

"He's gay."

"Same thing."

I stomp like a little girl. "No. It isn't."

He glares at me like it's all my fault somehow, that he's a bigoted freak, that Dylan is gay, that nothing is the way it should be. I point at him. "Don't look at me like that."

He shakes his head. "What happened to you, Belle? You used to be such a nice girl."

My mouth drops open. "I am a nice girl."

"Nice girls don't go out with fags," he takes a step closer. He looks away, looks back, his eyes soften for a second. "Why didn't you ever go out with me?"

Headlights motor down the street. They zip into my driveway and my sweet mom flounces out the car door. "Hey sweetie! Hey Eddie!"

She looks at both of us. "It's cold out here. Eddie, you want to come in?"

He shakes his head but just keeps staring at me. "No, thanks, Mrs. P. I've got homework to do."

"Okay, then." She reaches into the car to retrieve her purse and then starts walking toward me. "Bellie-bear, you coming inside?"

"Yep," I meet her on the walk and grab her hand.

Eddie calls after me. "I'll be seeing you, Belle."

I really don't hope so.

Tonight I pace around my house, do extra-credit homework, tell my mom I have too much studying to do so that if anyone calls can she tell them I'm already asleep?

She looks up from the newspaper. "Okay, honey."

Muffin takes that moment of distraction to pounce into the middle of the editorial page and settles herself in. My mother shakes her head, scratches at her hair with her pen, and laughs. "You little nuisance."

Muffin just looks up at her and purrs.

My mom scratches her beneath the chin and says to me, "You haven't been practicing guitar."

"I've been too busy," I lie.

She gives me a look that tells me she's not falling for that one. She stands up, catches me in a hug. I hug her back, just rest into her softness, inhale the smell of lilac and baked potatoes.

"It's so hard to be seventeen," she says into my hair. This is an eye-rolling comment, but I don't pull away first. She always says that she needs me to hug because I'm all the family she's got left, which is true, but a lot of responsibility and sometimes I just want to pull away, but I don't. I don't because I know how much that can hurt. Dylan taught me that.

She puts a little space between us so that she can look into my face. Her eyes glisten with worry.

"I saw Chief Tanner today," she says.

The shock does make me pull away. I pick up Muffin, snuggle her into my chest. "Yeah?"

"He told me about Dylan."

Everything inside me flares red and Muffin jumps out of my arms and scoots under the table. "Great, Mom. Just what I need. An inquisition. Are you going to ask me how I didn't know he was gay? I don't know . . . I just didn't, okay. I'm obviously stupid."

"Oh, sweetie," her arms reach out, but I duck away. "You aren't stupid."

"Yeah, right." I start folding up her newspaper, putting it all back together. The ink rubs off on my fingers. She's started a Sudoku puzzle, but hasn't finished it. She's given up partway.

"It's normal to be hurting, Belle."

I glare at her. "I am not hurting!"

I try to stomp by her, but she grabs me by the arm, traps me, pulls me in against her. "Sweetie, it's okay to hurt."

I let out some sort of inhuman yell, yank myself free, and storm off into my bedroom like a complete jerk. I throw myself onto my bed, glare at Gabriel waiting for me to play her, and then give up, pull my covers over my head and cry.

----o----

She comes into my room later and shuts off the light. She sits on the edge of my bed and smoothes my hair out of my face.

"Belle, I know you're not really asleep," she says.

I don't answer, just keep my eyes shut.

"You know, Eastbrook is a small place, honey, and everybody knows everybody's business and this whole Dylan thing is probably going to embarrass you for a bit, and hurt for awhile, but people will come around, honey. They won't hold it against you, and Dylan . . . well, Dylan, they'll come to accept him and love him again too. Really."

People like Eddie Caron. I almost laugh.

I open my eyes. My mother's face is shadowed in the dark of my room. Her breath smells like coffee. I keep my eyes open and wonder how I can love someone so sweet and so incredibly dumb. "People are mean, Mom," I tell her. "People are really, really mean."

The words hit her like fists and she tightens up, trying to escape the blows. Then her back solids up, her fingers turn to steel against my cheek. "No they aren't, Belle. I know how this town helped me out when your daddy died. They'll come through. I know they will."

She kisses my forehead and leaves. She doesn't slam my door, but I think she wants to. I can't blame her.

```
E-------3-----3----------------3---------|
A--------3-------3------------3----------|
D-----------0-----0---------0------------|
G-------------0-------2----X-------------|
B----------------X-------0----3----------|
E--------------------3-------X-----------|
```

Wednesday

I GET UP, STRETCH BIG and long, open my mouth, and think about singing. No sound comes out. My hand flutters up to my throat, grabbing it, like maybe that will some way, somehow make the words emerge into the darkness of my bedroom. Nothing.

My voice has vanished.

I trod over to the window, stub my toe on the nightstand, swear without making a sound since now I am soundless girl. Pulling up the shade, the outside word greets me with white crystals touching my window in patterns, patterns forming and overlapping with spikes and swirls, crystals as sparkling as diamonds. Jack Frost has visited over the night. That's what my mom would always say back when I was little. She'd pull up the shade, smash open the curtains, and with a smiling voice say, "Wake up, sleepy head. Jack Frost was here!"

"Here?" I'd say and struggle up to sit, knocking over the legions of stuffed animals, but never Teddy, my one-legged bear.

"Here," she'd say and come kiss the top of my head. "He came last night and he made you a picture."

Tears make pools in my eyes and my fingers trace the patterns. Why I'm so sad, I don't know. Jack Frost was here. He made me a picture and I can't even tell him how beautiful it is. I am soundless.

----o----

I can hear my mom singing all the way down the hall.

She's massacring lyrics again. She's singing that old Carly Simon song, "You're So Vain."

"I dreamed there were crowds in my potty, clowns in my potty," she croons.

The right lyrics are, of course, clouds in my coffee.

I schlump into the kitchen anyway. My mom stops singing, turns around with her sleep hair all crazy in the back, and smiles at me. She's got ready-made Postum in her hand and looks so sweet, like a movie mom. I smile at her and grab her hand, tugging her toward my bedroom.

"What, honey? What?" she asks me, but she doesn't resist, just lets me pull her down the hall.

"I want to show you something," I say, but no words come out.

"You've lost your voice?" She stops walking.

I nod and tug her hand. In my room I point at the window and the patterns of white lace, the images there, the magic.

"Oh," she says, her voice like a little girl's. "Jack Frost came."

She touches the window with the end of her long fingernail. I smile big at her. She smiles back. When she passes my guitar, she plucks the low E-string and the sound of it resonates off the Jack Frost window and around the room.

"You should start playing again," she says casually, as if it's nothing important, as if trying to make music isn't the hardest thing in the world.

----o----

Emily picks me up five minutes late. Her hair's still wet from the shower and cranky plasters her face.

"I overslept," she says, yawning.

I nod, grab her camera, and snap a picture of her. She gives me the finger.

She backs out of my driveway and my mom waves from the window and then grimaces, because Emily's little red car has come two inches from smashing over our mailbox. My mom spent the last five minutes pacing, combing her hair, sipping her coffee, pacing some more and pretty much chanting, "She's late. She's late. Is that girl ever on time? She's late. She's late. You are going to get another tardy."

Emily shifts into drive or forward or whatever it is that you shift cars into and peels down the road. I close my eyes and try not to imagine my mother's face. Now, she'll be praying, *Please don't let them get in an accident. Please don't let them get killed.*

"I finished my applications last night," Emily says. She yawns again. I catch it and play the yawn back to her. "So, I'm only a week behind you."

I finished mine last week, signed, sealed, and mailed. Bates. Smith. Cornell. Trinity. A ragtag assortment of schools. Emily's applying to Duke, Bucknell, Loyola, St. Joe's. Neither of us is applying to U Maine. Neither of us has a safe school. I figure Smith is my safety, or close enough. I'm proud of Emily for getting it done. She tends to be a late-fee kind of person, the kind of person who leaves her library books in the car for months, because she keeps forgetting to return them, the kind of person the video store calls and leaves threatening messages because she's had "She's All That" for three months.

"I applied to Bates last minute," Emily beams. "I'm really done, I swear."

"Good," I say, but my voice is barely a croaky whisper. I give her two big thumbs-up instead.

"Oh, you lost your voice," Emily says. "You sound sexy."

"Yeah, like a sexy frog," I try to say.

Emily leans over to hear me. "What?"

"Yeah, like a sexy frog," I repeat.

She holds up her hands, which should be on the steering wheel. "Don't talk. Let me do the talking."

She flashes me a wicked smile, rolls through the stop sign, and rushes right onto the Surry Road. A squirrel skitters out of her way.

"Well, I decided to apply to Bates, 'cause you guys all did," she blushes, inhales, and gets ready. "I think that Shawn is really, really cute and that he maybe likes me, which is cool, you know, as long as it isn't too hard on you with the whole Dylan deal and everything."

She looks to me. I smile big like a Wal-Mart sticker so that she'll continue. I'm not going to begrudge Emily any happiness, God knows she's been the third wheel with Dylan and me for way too many things.

"So, it's okay?" she asks.

I nod.

"So, we're going to the dance on Friday and I know you don't want to come but you have to come. You have to. I mean, I can't ignore, like the fact that Dylan is gay and everything and you've been to every single dance with him and stuff. But . . . well, I mean, now's the time for you to experience the boyfriendless high school angst that the rest of us have to deal with on a daily basis."

"Angst?" I croak out.

"SAT word," Emily blurts and we're almost there. If it wasn't so hard to talk, I'd tell her I know what angst means. Really. "Okay? So, it's not like you'll be standing up against the wall the whole time . . ."

I know she's thinking about the infamous eighth grade dance where I either hid from Eddie Caron or squatted by the Coke machine for the entire time.

"And I mean you did kiss Tom yesterday, so I'm not even sure you can count as boyfriendless . . . although, it's not like you guys are going out or anything. Although he is driving you to that German restaurant . . ."

Panic hits my stomach. I lean over.

"You okay?" she asks. "Are you sick sick or is it just your voice?"

I shake my head. I don't know. I don't know what's wrong with me other than I'm scared to go to a stupid dance without Dylan holding my hand, making me not have to worry about slow dances and annoying guys with too-hot roaming hands and just letting myself go into the bang bang of the beat and the smooth moves of the music. That's all gone now. That's dead. And Tom . . . Tom's kiss? Oh, God, that made me feel like I was on fire, in a very,

very good way and the guilt of that is huge and just vibrates against my soul like a plucked E-string, low and grating.

"Will Dylan be there?" I ask Emily.

She takes a second to understand what I've said and then her eyebrows lift up. She turns into the parking lot. "With Bob? Oh my God, I don't know. Do you think they're that brave?"

I shrug.

"He did wear that pink triangle yesterday and buy those freaking condoms, in front of Dolly and everything," Emily parks, barely missing the fender of a black pickup truck. She stares at me. "Oh, you poor baby. Your life sucks."

Nodding, I unbuckle my seat belt and Emily pushes me out the door. "Now, haul your ass out of my car and run, 'cause we are both wicked late."

EM TAKES A PICTURE OF me running to school. I look frantic. My backpack swings out from my shoulder. My hair tangles behind me. My mouth tights itself into my face. I look like a girl who has never plucked a guitar, a girl who never sings.

LAW CLASS. MR. RICHTER RUSHES in ten minutes after we all get there. Emily and I have escaped a tardy.

The first five minutes Mr. Richter didn't show up, we all sat in our chairs and were good kids. We waited and wondered where Mr. Punctual was, but after awhile it just became party time. Emily swished over and sat on Shawn's desk. Anna, Andrew, and Kara tried to talk to me about Dylan and his "newly discovered" gayness, but I couldn't say anything with no voice and everyone eventually gave up.

So, I put my head down on the desk and wait, wait, wait for something to happen. Every once in awhile, when I poke my head up, Mimi Cote stares at me and picks at her nails. I shiver. I try to clear my throat. Even with everything, I am so glad that Dylan picked me, sang stupid songs with me, and not her.

Mr. Richter finally bangs in, his hair standing up straight and tie whacked to the side.

"People," he says with an elaborate sigh, leaning against his desk, hands on his narrow hips. "You will never believe what was in my swimming pool."

"Ronald McDonald!" Emily yells as she scrambles off Shawn's desk and back to her seat.

He shakes his head.

"A stripper!" someone shouts out. Shawn, I think.

He rolls his eyes. "No. Two moose."

We say nothing.

He points a finger in the air. "Two gay moose. They were mating or whatever gay moose do."

Shocked silence. Then Emily says, "In your swimming pool?"

Mr. Richter shakes his head. "They tore the liner to bits."

Emily makes eyes at me. I nod. We think the same thing. Is everybody in the world gay? And no one's told us.

"Even the moose," she mouths at me.

I mouth it back. "Even the moose."

"Do you think they wore condoms?" she mouths.

I twitch my nose at her and she smiles.

"Eww," says Mimi, trying to pull her miniskirt down, despite the fact that she's sitting on it. "That's sick."

Em does a perfect Mimi-twisted face impression behind her back and I start laughing so hard I have to put my head back down on my desk.

Mr. Richter uses Mimi's comment to start a debate about sexuality and privacy rights. He tells us about a case where two men were in their own house having sex and they were arrested for sodomy.

"In some states," Mr. Richter points his pencil at us, "it is illegal for men to engage in anal sex. In some states it is illegal for a man and a woman to engage in oral sex."

Someone makes a gagging noise, but Shawn raises his hand and squeaks out, "Not here, right?"

Mr. Richter nods.

Emily can't help herself. "You're safe, Shawn."

Shawn crosses his arm, shakes his head, leans back in his chair, and smiles.

DYLAN, DO YOU KNOW HOW *dangerous the world is for you?*
Do you know that your kind of love is against the law? When
I think your name, I become an ache. You were my best
friend. You are my best friend.

I miss you.

I've written you a lot of notes since Saturday, but this one
I'm going to give you.

You're gay, I've got it. So what? So let's be us still, Dylan
and Belle, best of friends, harmony and melody, show tune
and folk song, friends, soul swappers, okay?

I WAIT OUTSIDE HIS MATH class like some sort of stalker. I wave to people I know. Shawn and Em walk by and he pets my head like I'm some sort of puppy dog. And then Dylan trots down the hall. There's no pink triangle on his shirt today. His face wears shadows and suspicion. His head darts to the side, looking for predators, behind him, I think.

"Dylan," my word is one note, one note in the hall.

He sees me. "Belle."

My lips turn up into a slow smile. His mouth flashes brilliant teeth. He comes close, in my space, really, like he's still a boyfriend. Boy. Friend. He is.

"You're in my personal space," I laugh at my half-there voice and my half-there joke.

He jerks back and starts to apologize, but I grab his sleeve. "No, I'm teasing."

He smiles again. Some kid excuses himself and pushes by us, but really slow, 'cause he wants to hear what's going on. "You lost your voice?"

I shrug and fish inside my pocket. I refuse to think about condoms. "I wrote you a note."

He takes it. Our fingers brush, but there's no super-electric funky sparks. I swallow. Dylan looks at the paper.

"It's okay," I croak. "It's not mean or angry or anything."

He nods. He clears his throat. Someone else pushes by and Dylan says, "I never meant to hurt you, Belle."

His green-grass eyes water like rain is stuck there.

"I know," I whisper say with my almost voice. "Me either."

By the time I climb into Tom's truck, my voice is back, which is good and bad, because now I have to talk to Tom with his black truck and sin eyes and man-low voice. I don't know what to say.

"Thanks for the ride," I manage as he shifts. My lips twitch, remembering lip things that they shouldn't be remembering. Bad lips.

He shrugs. "Like I said, I didn't want to have to bring Crash or Bob."

There's duct tape on the steering wheel, duct tape on the seat, and a little duct tape man standing on the dash, forever kicking a little duct tape soccer ball that's attached to his foot.

I touch the duct tape man with my pinky finger. Tom turns on the ignition and says, "Ready."

"For a fun night of German food, yum. Yippee," I deadpan.

He laughs.

His truck smells like him, deodorant and soap, clean and musky, but with just a bit of burnt marshmallow mixed in. It smells like man. Dylan never smelled like man. He smelled like pine woods and grass. Why didn't I notice that? Why didn't I notice things?

Herr Reitz, who smells like halitosis and bologna, skips up to our car and hands us a map of where to go. "Just in case you get lost."

Tom raises his eyebrows because how long have all of

us lived in this town? All our lives. And how often do we go to Bangor? Every week. "That's a good idea."

I nod in an overenthusiastic way and Tom presses his lips together to keep from laughing.

Herr Reitz fake scowls at us, points his finger. "No hanky panky, you two."

Then he winks.

My cheeks turn scarlet. My hands touch the hotness of them. Tom shakes his head. "What a freak."

I nod. Herr Reitz bounces on his toes, giving a girl named Janelle a map. Her car is crammed with people. I am sure there are not enough seat belts to go around. Bob is riding with Herr Reitz. I feel sorry for him.

Herr Reitz finally gets into his car and toots out a happy little beep.

"Finally," Tom breathes out. He takes his foot off the brake, eases down the parking lot.

His thighs fill out his jeans. I close my eyes, lean my head against the back of the seat. "You already sick of me?"

My voice betrays my heart and it comes out sad and pathetic.

"Sick of my pinko commie friend," he laughs. "Never."

I open my eyes to make sure I don't miss when I punch him in the arm. He just laughs harder and yells, "Assault! Assault! I've been attacked by a peacenik hippie freak."

I raise my eyebrows at him. He turns on the radio, not to something loud, like I expect from those over-adrenalined soccer player rich boys, but something chocolate-cake smooth, old soul music from our grandparents' days. I raise my eyebrows at him again and then wonder if they'll get stuck there. Maybe I should plaster some duct tape over them.

"What?" His hands leave the steering wheel. "I like Marvin Gaye."

He winces.

"It's okay," I say. "Gay is the theme of my life."

"You're not?" he blurts out.

"Hardly."

"I didn't think so," he says and I know he's remembering the couch incident, just the same way I'm remembering it. I try to push that memory down the heating vent but then he smiles at me. My heart flitters like dragonflies and I decide that the window view of barren Maine trees is worth contemplating.

"How about you?"

He coughs. "God, no."

"Did you always know that Dylan was?" I ask him.

He takes a minute. We drive past Eastbrook Building Supplies and Friend, where they sell motorcycles and ATVs. He pulls in a deep breath and says, "Not always. I figured it out in eighth grade."

"What?" I sit up straighter. My heart leaps away from my lungs.

"Remember that deal I told you about?"

"Yeah."

Mrs. Foster, the city councilor who is afraid Wal-Mart

might come, drives by in her Subaru and honks at us. Tom honks back. We both smile. That's what you do in Eastbrook unless you want people talking about you.

Tom gets back to the point. "Well, right before the pact, we went to the Sea Coast Fun Park and he tried to kiss me. I mean, I'm pretty sure he did but he didn't make it."

That means Dylan always knew.

"Jesus," my heart pounds. "All the way back in eighth grade?"

"Yeah."

"Did you freak?"

He nods. That muscle in his cheek spasms and against my will my finger reaches up and touches it. I feel a little twitch beneath my fingertip. I take my finger away, pat him on the shoulder, and he keeps talking. "I was scared shitless. After that, Dylan made a very big deal about liking girls, like he was proving it to both of us, you know. And then Mimi asked me out and so . . ."

I nod and twist my hand in my lap. "And so . . ."

His little duct tape man stays stuck on the dashboard even as we pound into a pothole. I stare and stare at him, thinking how great it would be to be stuck and cemented, to know where you are, where you're supposed to be, a duct tape man with a little soccer ball.

"You doing okay?" Tom asks after a minute.

"Yeah." I inhale and take the time to look at him. His chin juts out straight and strong like superheroes in those old black-and-white movies, like cowboys. His skin glows the color of good tree bark. I gulp.

Inside my body, tree limbs stretch out, scraping at my skin. That's all there is in there. No leaves. No fruit. Maybe it's not even tree limbs, but the branches of blueberry bushes, barren and aching. But when I look at Tom, it feels like things are sprouting, like they're getting ready to grow and fill me.

"You scared me when you fainted the other day," he smiles. "I'm sorry . . . passed out."

My hands clasp each other. "Sorry."

"No big." His cheeks redden. "You're okay now, right?"

I nod. "Yeah."

"You sure?"

"Yeah."

His free hand picks up the roll of duct tape and tosses it onto the floor. "I was worried about you."

"About a pinko commie hippie freak?" I tease and then bite the inside of my lip. I want to pluck the little duct tape man off the dash and put him in my pocketbook with my guitar.

He breathes in through his nose and when he breathes out it's just one word. "Yeah."

I smile. I move my hair behind my ear and then wonder if that's a flirty thing to do, touching your hair? Em would know.

"What do you think about the Eddie Caron thing?"

he asks as we turn onto Bangor Road. Janelle passes us and honks. A million hands reach out her windows and give us the finger. Tom laughs and waves his middle digit back.

"What Eddie Caron thing?"

He puts his hand back on the steering wheel. His knuckles pale. "You don't know?"

I shake my head. A branch scrapes up against my lung and I cough.

His Adam's apple moves down in his throat then comes back up. "He said he's going to beat the crap out of Dylan."

"He what?" My ears explode. I turn off Marvin Gaye singing about getting it on. "Why?"

Tom's eyes stop watching the back of Janelle's car and kind into me. "You know why, Belle."

"Because he's gay?" My voice gives out, midsentence, but Tom understands.

Tom nods and his voice comes out steady, "He's pissed 'cause Dylan and Bob are going to the dance."

My hands shake so I clamp them together on my lap. "Together?"

"Yeah."

I take this in. We climb up a hill. My chest feels like it's my legs not Tom's truck doing all the work.

"Should I pass them?" Tom nods toward Janelle's car.

It's a big hill. It's a no passing zone. "Yeah."

I open my window and cold wind bursts in, whipping my hair. Tom yells, "Yee-haw" as we roar by. The truck's transmission whines. I wave my finger in the air and close the window.

"You gave them the finger," Tom says, laughing.

"Didn't you want me to?"

"Yeah, but I never imagined you giving anyone the finger."

"There's a lot about me you probably would never have imagined."

"Oh, I wouldn't bet."

There's no mistaking what he means. I turn red again. I cough. Something inside me blooms. Tom grabs my hand and says all mellow, "Everything'll be okay."

"With Dylan?"

He shrugs. "Yeah. With Dylan. But mostly with you. Everything will be good. I promise."

Part of me wants to ask him how he knows, but a bigger part of me, the part that wins out, just wants to believe him. That part holds his hand tighter and doesn't worry about anything, just focuses on the warmth of it, how much bigger his fingers are than mine, twice the size. His hand feels nothing like Dylan's hand, which was small like mine, but it feels good, Tom's hand. It feels really good like branches swaddled with leaves and little duct tape men knowing where to be.

- - - - o - - - -

At the German restaurant, I find Bob and corner him by a

giant replica of some Bavarian hussy with monster boobs and equally oversized beer steins.

"Have you heard about Eddie Caron?" I ask him.

"Yeah."

He wipes his thick glasses, which have fogged up because the air in here is humid like at the Y pool.

I glare at him. "Does Dylan know?"

He shrugs. "We're not worried about it Belle, we'll take him."

"You'll *take* him?" I echo.

My mouth drops open and thick-glasses, no-muscles Bob says, "I got to go find a seat. I don't want to get stuck with Herr Reitz."

"You've never been in a fight you're whole entire life," I hoarse shout after him.

He whirls around. "Every day in my life is a fight, Belle."

He lets that sink in and then says, "And Damien Derr stuck my head in a toilet once."

"That doesn't count," I say. "That was second grade."

Tom walks up beside me, puts his arm around my shoulder, and steers me to a table. "It counts. Believe me. It counts."

"Eddie Caron is huge," I say, my fingers trembling. "He'll kill them."

Tom nods and sits down across from me. His foot stretches out under the table and hooks under my ankle. "It'll be okay."

My foot tingles and then rests next to his. It feels good and warm and safe. Will Dylan ever be warm and safe?

Will Bob? I put my napkin in my lap. Tom tucks his into his shirt collar, but I glare at him. He laughs and snaps it out like a waiter and then puts it in his lap, too.

"Just teasing," he says.

Herr Reitz stands up at the end of the table. He's changed into some bright pink lederhosen. He claps his hands.

"No songs!" Crash shouts. "Not in public!"

Herr Reitz puts on a fake sad face. "How about God Bless America?"

We all groan.

He smiles and claps his hands again. "Okay. Everyone! Let the festivities begin!"

A waitress with neither beer steins nor enormous breasts plops a big plate of bratwurst and sauerkraut in front of me, waiting for me to pick up my fork and cut into it, break it into pieces, devour it, until there's nothing left but crumbs. It will wait a long, long time.

Eddie Caron is bratwurst fingers, squinty mean eyes, and YMCA muscles. He is not a guy you want to tangle with. I mean, we used to be bus friends when we were little, which was great and he was always, always, always protecting me from the big-kid bullies. He'd fight anybody, anybody, all the time.

All dinner, I think about Eddie Caron's bratwurst fingers connected to his hammer hands and tree-trunk muscles. I imagine those hands that used to build me dirt castles hitting Dylan, lean, golden Dylan. Dylan with the clear skin. Blonde hair mats with blood. Golden skin turns green and black and broken.

I can't even swallow my cider.

"Eat up, Fraulien," Herr Reitz yells at me from down the table. A glob of sauerkraut sticks in his beard, hanging there, a pale worm clinging in a mass of brown. I shudder.

Herr Reitz raises his non-alcoholic Feuerzangenbowle. All the guys look at it with envy eyes. "Belle, eat! You'll get too skinny!"

I stab the bratwurst with my fork and he smiles.

"Yummy bratwurst!" Crash kids, making his soar near my mouth the way a mom does when she's trying to get a little kid to eat peas or something. "Open up. Here comes the airplane. Let's open the hanger."

I crack up. There's nothing else to do.

----o----

If you can tell a man by his car then Tom Tanner is solid and safe with big tires, a lot of duct tape holding him together, and a moderate amount of chrome. His fenders are a little dirty and he likes to drive fast; if Tom is his truck then he is comfortable and he holds you high enough that you can get a good view of the world around you, at the other cars passing by, the ambulance blaring out somebody's sad emergency, the broken-down van that's parked on the grass with the hood open.

I am just a passenger. I am along from the ride. I crack some non-aspartame gum that I'm using to get the taste of German food out of my mouth. The gum is stale already. Gum without aspartame gets stale in two seconds. I put another piece in. Tom blows a bubble and pops it. I scooch up against the back of the seat and position myself so I'm sitting Indian style.

We've picked up a hitchhiker, sort of. Crash said he couldn't stand it in Herr Reitz's car anymore and he'd have to commit suicide by bratwurst if he was forced to drive back in Herr Reitz's geekmobile. Tom took pity. So, we're crunched three in the long front seat of the cab, and Crash lives up to his name, two times. First, he crashes his way into Tom's truck. Second, he crashes in the truck, just plummets off some high cliff of consciousness into the deep oblivion of la-la land. His head rests against the window. Snores tumble out of his open mouth.

"Jesus," Tom mutters and keeps driving.

"He sounds like elephants," I whisper.

"More like someone farting out their mouth," Tom shakes his head. "I am never driving anyone home again. Serves me right for being nice."

I close my eyes, lean my head back. "How about me?"

"What about you?"

Crash lets out a mighty honk.

"Are you ever going to drive me home again?" I ask. My palms tingle. Too soon. Too soon to feel this way, I know. Too soon.

Tom grabs my hand in his. His fingers wrap around it and a shiver starts in my belly, works its way through me. He keeps my hand under his and puts both on the steering wheel. We're driving together, sort of. His hand holds mine between his warm fingers and the cold steering wheel.

"You," he says. "You, pinko, commie girl, I'd take anywhere."

----o----

The night darkens all the familiar territory around us. There aren't a lot of streetlamps, even on Route 1A, so we navigate by the yellow line in the middle of the road and our guts, trusting that they will tell us the right way.

A big, low plane flashes its red lights just above the tree line. Judging from the size, it's probably a Navy cargo plane that's just taken off from Bangor. I wonder if Tom likes planes.

"I don't know everything about you," I whisper because even though Crash is snoring, I'm afraid he'll hear.

Tom squeezes my hand beneath his. "Like what?"

"Like your favorite food."

"My favorite food."

"Yeah."

He lifts up his hand and a finger traces across my skin. "Parsnips and oranges."

"You're kidding."

He shrugs and smiles. "I like parsnips. They're sort of snappy and fresh."

"Like you."

He laughs. "Like me."

My hand tingles. His finger traces patterns on it. His other hand is firmly planted on the steering wheel. The duct tape man on the dashboard smiles at me. He must know that everything inside me tingles.

"Why oranges?" I ask, my voice turns husky somehow. It betrays me.

"I like the juice when they're really fresh and you bite into them. They're sweet." He takes his hand away and waves it in the air.

"Yeah, but when you bite into them they squirt you in the eye," I say, and pull my hand off the steering wheel. It rests on my lap, useless.

"That's the chance you've got to take," he says.

A memory surfaces. "You used to share your oranges with me, back in first grade or something. Do you remember?"

Tom nods. The plane disappears, obscured by the roof of the truck. I remember out loud, "And your mom cut them into quarters or something. And you would always give me a piece at recess. We'd stand by the swings and we'd chomp on those oranges."

I pout. "They always squirted me in the eye."

Tom laughs. "I know and you'd always get so mad and the juice would dribble on your chin and you'd wipe at it with your sleeve, squinting."

"Attractive."

"It was."

I harrumph. "Then you'd push Mimi and me on the swings but only a couple times because you'd always take off and play soccer on the far field."

He doesn't say anything. Crash crashes out a particularly loud snore.

"Do you remember that?" I ask, my voice down to a whisper again. I want so badly for him to remember.

"I never forgot," he says.

We drive a little more and pass County Ambulance zooming to Maine Coast Memorial Hospital. Its red lights flash out emergency messages.

"I should get you an orange," Tom says. He grabs my hand and holds it in his and it feels like home, and first-grade swings and the juice of oranges that explode sweet against your tongue.

- - - - o - - - -

We drop Crash off at his big mansion house on the Union River and shake him awake.

He nods at us in a real, lazy way and then like someone's flicked a switch he turns back on his hyper self. "Dude, thanks for the ride."

He hops out of the car, leaving Tom and I laughing as he does a front handspring up his driveway.

"I can't believe he called you 'Dude,'" I say.

Tom laughs and shifts it into gear as I start to slide across the seat. He reaches across to me with his hand and says, "Where you going, Commie?"

"Dude, I was going to give your dude-like self some more dude room," I say.

He pulls me back, slow, steady and leans down. His lips are dangerously close to my lips and he says, "I don't need any room."

- - - - o - - - -

We decide it's early and that we should go to the Y and work out, which seems like some sort of commitment, working out together, but I don't think about it as I slam up the stairs, past my mom, and into my room to grab some clothes and my sneakers.

She stalls me in the hall, blocking my way, hands on her hips, but a smile on her face. "Where you going?"

"The Y," I say.

She nods, kisses my forehead. "Emily bringing you?"

"Tom."

Her mouth twitches like she's trying not to smile. My mouth twitches the same exact way. "Tom? Tom Tanner?"

I nod and move by her. "Uh-huh."

"Well, have fun and don't be home late," she laughs and I turn around and she's got this full-blown monster smile plastered on her face like she thinks I am a very funny person, very amusing indeed.

"Mom?" I throw at her to let her know she's amusing too. "You know that 'Piña Colada' song you're always singing?"

"Yeah," Muffin twines herself between my mother's legs.

"The line is not, 'I am humping chimp's pain.' It's 'I am into champagne.'"

She smiles, flushes, and points at me. "That's good to know."

I shake my head and barrel down the stairs and out the door.

- - - - o - - - -

The Eastbrook Y is not one of those fancy Ys like in big cities. There's a gym but no indoor track. There's a pool but it's about the size of a pool in a nice hotel. The roof leaks. The paint on the walls peels and the floor is always dirty. But the people who work there—Janine, Shane, and Mike—are all great. They love kids. They've taught every Eastbrook kid the right way to drain a jumper or kick a soccer ball.

It's Janine manning the front desk when Tom and I walk in. She's the one who explained to my crying four-year-old self that it doesn't hurt your toes if you remember to kick the soccer ball with the side of your foot instead of the front. She's a sweetie, everybody in town was ready to lynch her husband when he ran off with Janine's sixteen-year-old niece a couple years back. He motored up to the drive-thru at McDonald's where the niece worked, ordered a Big Mac and a side of scumbag. They drove off together and never looked back. You can't tell that by looking at

Janine though. She's all smiles and raised eyebrows as Tom and I give her our ID cards, which is pointless, because everybody knows everybody anyway.

"Well, well, well," she says, handing our cards back. "Tom Tanner and Belle Philbrick, it's about time you two showed up here together."

I blush red but Tom just says, "Tell me about it."

Janine says, "Do you two remember back when you were in Mighty Mites soccer and Dylan side-tackled Belle because he wanted the ball even though they were on the same team?"

I shake my head, totally confused, but Tom nods.

Janine starts laughing. "You don't remember this, Belle?"

She doesn't wait for my answer. I shift the weight of my gym bag onto my shoulder and Tom reaches out and takes it while Janine keeps talking. "Tom runs over like a little paramedic, wipes the dirt off your calf, yells at me to get you an icepack, and then side-tackles Dylan as soon as play started again."

She nods at Tom. "How old were you then?"

He lifts his shoulders up, and the gym bags move with him. "Six? Seven?"

"I had you two pegged for a couple way back then," she sighs and shakes her head at us like we're dimwits. "I can't believe it took you so long."

Tom grabs my hand and squeezes it.

Janine gives me cougar eyes and I'm locked there by the front desk of the Y. Basketball sounds emanate from behind the closed doors of the gym. It's Wednesday night men's league. I think Tom's dad plays in that. I want to look away toward the doors but I can't. I'm a deer caught in the headlights of Janine's knowing eyes. That's the problem with Eastbrook, everybody has knowing eyes.

"You never should have given up soccer," she says to me and I know what she means. I never should have given up a lot of things. I think about Gabriel at home, waiting for me to play her. I think about Tom, standing right next to me, holding my hand. I think about Dylan's friendship.

I can have all those things. I can.

"Thanks, Janine," I say to her and her eyes register some sort of knowledge that has passed between us.

"Anytime, Belle dear, anytime."

----o----

When I come out of the locker room, sounds of angry male voices thunder at me from the fitness room down the hall. I'm not the sort of person who likes fights, especially between weight-lifting steroid heads, so I pivot back toward the locker room and almost go back in. That's when I hear it. My name.

"Crap," I mutter and run into the fitness room, yanking open the door. Janine, who has pumps on and a skirt, is right behind me.

We both stop, stunned, when we get inside.

Tom and Dylan square off over by the squat machine. Tom's hands spread apart like he's trying to talk down a mad dog. Dylan's sputters and his fists wait in the air.

I stagger backwards and Janine catches me, leans me against the wall, and strides toward them, stomping over one of those white towels people use to wipe down the equipment. Tom and Dylan don't even notice her.

"I swear I'll freaking kill you," Dylan growls. He's hunched and circling Tom like he's ready to lash out.

"Jesus, Dylan. Calm down." Tom glares at him, with hate in his eyes.

"Me calm down? Why don't you fucking calm down?"

"Shut the hell up, Dylan."

"You shut up."

If there wasn't the threat of violence involved I would laugh because their dialogue is that stupid. I have no idea what they're angry about. I have never seen either of them in a fight. Oh, that's not true. Tom slugged Brandon Bartlett in fourth grade because Brandon pulled my hair. That was sort of gallant of him.

But I don't want them to fight, not Tom and Dylan, not here, not now, not ever.

"Guys!" I yell, but they don't even know I'm here. They just keep glaring, clenching fists, circling. The anger fills up the entire fitness room and people are paying attention, stopping their sets, slowing down on the cardio machines.

Dylan stands up straight and his lips are lines that do not hold in his anger. "You moved right in, didn't you? What? We were broken up a day?"

"Shut up," Tom takes a step toward him.

"Yeah, the only way you could ever get her was if she was rebounding. Big stud Tom Tanner. You were just waiting, weren't you?"

For a moment neither of them move. For a moment neither of them say anything. Somebody behind me clangs a weight on the floor.

"You and Bob were making out in the parking lot Sunday so don't give me crap about moving too fast." Tom nods over toward the free weights and there's Bob hanging by the wall looking stunned and angry. A ten-pound weight dangles from his hand. He had absolutely no muscle tone. Not that that's important. No, what's important is that the two guys in my life are snarling at each other like wild dogs and I swear I don't recognize either of them.

Janine walks closer.

"Boys," her voice is a warning they don't hear.

"What about the pact?" Dylan asks, standing up straighter. "You promised."

"Fuck that." Tom shakes his head, straightens up too, his hands come down. "Fuck the pact. You screwed it up first."

Dylan rushes him, throwing a right hook. Tom tries to dodge but the ab machine's in his way and Dylan's fist smashes into the side of Tom's face. I jerk back like I'm the one who has been hit and try to rush forward but other people are gathering around them, rushing off the cardio machines, now that it's a real full-blown fight. There's the guy from the radiology department at the lab who just moved to town moving in front of me. There's my fifth-grade science teacher, Mr. Key, holding his hands out in some sort of pleading peace gesture. They're all telling Dylan and Tom to settle down. But it just seems to make them both angrier.

"How did I break it first?" Dylan yells. I can hear a fist hit something, but I can't see over the people and I can't get past the radiology guy, who is holding me back.

"Stop it, boys," yells Mr. Key.

"By what? By being gay?" Dylan says. Then he makes an oophing noise that means Tom's hit him back. Everything inside my body shakes, like the earth's given way, like even my organs, my muscles, my bones have lost all stability.

Several people pull in their breath.

"I don't give a shit about you being gay," Tom says.

"Then what?"

Janine smashes by me and says, "I'm going to go get Tom's dad. He's in the gym. Don't let them hurt each other."

Like that's possible. Still, I nod and manage to get past radiology man just as Tom says, "No, when you and Mimi hooked up sophomore year."

I stagger and almost fall. My world spins. Mimi? Mr. Key grabs my arm and whispers my name but I shake him off and go to stand behind Tom. Dylan cheated on me. With Mimi. When we were sophomores? Was this before or after we were going out?

Tom looks like he wants to spit at Dylan and according to my reflection in the big mirror on the way, I look that way too.

Dylan's eyes glance past Tom and at me. His anger crumples. His fists turn back into hands with fingers. He is not golden, but yellow. Tom shakes his head, "You always had to have it all, Dylan, but you can't. You can't have it all. No one can."

Dylan looks up to the sky. His Adam's apple moves along his throat like he's gulping for air and my heart aches for him, despite everything. He murmurs to the ceiling, "I don't want it all."

I step in front of Tom and grab Dylan by the shoulders, forcing him to look at me. Tears rest in the corners of his eyes and my voice comes out soft, "Then what is it you want, Dylan?"

His lip trembles. His eyes look past mine, at Tom, at the crowd and he says in an almost whisper, "To be myself."

"Oh, sweetie," I say and hug him close. Over his shoulder Bob's ears turn red, so I let Dylan go just as Tom storms away, out of the gym and into the hall. I turn and watch him go. My arms feel empty though. My arms still feel like they need to hug someone, maybe Tom, maybe Dylan.

Dylan wipes at his eyes and Bob drops his weight on the floor. Behind me Mr. Key says, "Okay, everybody. Nothing more to see."

Tom and Dylan and I, though, we aren't done yet. Tom's not anyway. All his dad's cop-authority training must have rubbed off on him somehow because he stomps back in, charging like a bull or something and he reaches out a hand, grabs Dylan's upper arm and says like he means it, "But you can't hurt other people. You can't push them aside in your quest to be you."

Dylan nods and something solids his eyes. "You either."

Tom lets go and spreads out his own arms like they are wings. He agrees. "Me either."

Tom's dad comes in a second later. And even though he's wearing basketball shorts and a sleeveless shirt instead of his uniform, he takes Dylan aside and starts lecturing him in that calm, stable way he has. He is, I am sure, telling him to be careful. He glares at Tom, points at him, and says in a total dad way, "I'll talk to you at home."

Tom and I go out to the hall and down a corner where no one can see us. I lean against the wall and Tom stands in front of me. My whole body shakes against the cold concrete blocks that somebody's painted blue and white in an attempt to make the Y look nicer, I guess.

"Belle?" His voice is a question mixed with a want.

It is all I can do not to cry. The whole Dylan and Mimi thing is too much, after everything else. I wonder if everyone knew, or just Tom and why Tom never told me. Because of some stupid pact?

A gulp lodges in my throat and I push it back and say, "Why didn't you ever tell me?"

"You would have hated me. You would've thought I was just trying to break you guys up because I was jealous."

I shake my head. My voice is angry. "You don't know that."

"Yeah, I do. Belle . . ."

I press my lips tight and don't bend. Tom's eyes flash in anger. "You didn't have to hug him in there."

"He was hurt." I glare at him and then realize he's hurt too. There's a cut on his forehead, near his temple that's bleeding and the whole area is swelling.

"You're hurt." I reach up my hand and let it rest on Tom's head, like I could magically take away the pain, just make the injury go away. My eyes stare into his and I can see the anger fade out, fade away like a plane moving past the horizon of the sky. "I don't like him that way. I'm not sure how I ever liked him that way, but I don't like him that way now."

"And what about me?" His voice is mellow and harsh, rough and bumpy like a tree trunk, but whole somehow too, strong, holding up the weight of an entire tree.

I don't move my hand away as I say, "I like you, Tom. I really like you, but it's so quick and I'm so scared. That sounds wimpy. I know that sounds wimpy."

I shake my head and drop my hand, start to turn away. "I was so wrong about Dylan. I don't want to be wrong like that again."

He leans toward me, puts his hands on either sides of my shoulders, and stares at me with serious tree-bark eyes. "I swear, I'll never hurt you."

I shake my head, breaking. "You can't know that."

He cups my hand in his chin. "Yes, yes I can."

WE SIT IN HIS TRUCK, parked outside my house. Every once in a while my mom walks in front of the living room window and peeks out at us, thinking she's all discreet.

"My mom's watching," I laugh.

Tom looks at me, chews on his lip a bit, and then starts fiddling with his duct tape, twisting it fast and furious. "I never understood why you started playing guitar in grade school. Was it to make Dylan like you?"

"No." I watch his fingers instead of his face, try to figure out what he's making. "It's because I like stories."

His fingers stop for a second. "Stories?"

"Yeah, stories. I like songs that are stories and I like to tell them, I guess," I pull up my shoe and start trying to unwedge a pebble that's stuck in the tread.

Tom rips off a piece of duct tape, grabs my shoe, and sticks the tape on the bottom. He smiles at me, slow and long. "Watch."

With one quick movement, he rips the tape off. Stuck to it is the pebble.

"Wow," I say. I grab the duct tape and look at all the dirt and tiny rocks stuck on it now, lint that I've walked over, lint that's stuck to me and I never noticed it the whole time it was tagging along.

"Why not write stories then?" he asks me, leaning back. The truck's overhead light makes him glow a little, which reminds me of Dylan, which reminds me of Dylan and him fighting in the Y.

The cut on his face by his ear has stopped bleeding,

but the swelling all around it hasn't gone down. I reach out toward it but don't touch. "Does that hurt?"

He shakes his head. "You're avoiding the question."

"I know, but I think I should get you some ice."

"Only wimps need ice. Answer my question."

"Okay, He-Man. I like words out loud better," I say. "Sometimes stories seem pretentious and I'm not so good at getting to the music under the words when I just have a paper and a pen, or on the computer, you know . . . It's different somehow."

He shifts closer. "I'm listening."

"The thing is, a songwriter is part of history. They are part of this tradition of singing other people's stories, and their own stories, too, obviously. Like, if you look at old songs, they are tools for understanding history of people. Not just the presidents and the hoity-toity academics and stuff, but the regular people."

He nods and shuts off the overhead light. An owl hoots outside somewhere. A dog barks its response. The lights in Eddie Caron's house flicker like the furnace has come on.

"And every time you sing a song, you change it a little, you leave your mark. Pete Seeger, this famous folk guy, he said that." I shift on the seat. "That sounded pretentious before, didn't it? Saying songs are 'tools for understanding.' That's so pretentious."

I shake my head because sometimes I am stupid.

"You worry too much about being pretentious," Tom says. "You are the least pretentious person I know."

"Really?"

"Really. Pretentious people do not wear Snoopy shoes."

I admire them. "Do you think they're stupid? They aren't exactly the height of fashion."

He smiles and tugs at one of my laces, untying it. "I think they're you."

"Dylan hated them. So I never wore them. I've had them forever."

"They're cute." He closes his eyes for a second the way people do when their head hurts.

"You sure you don't want some ice?" I ask.

"Nah, I have to go home soon."

"Your dad going to kill you?"

He opens his eyes again and smiles like it doesn't matter. "Probably."

His eyes are so intense and deep and dangerous that I have to look away. Across the street, Eddie's body is silhouetted in the light of his living room window. He's moved the drapes and is staring out into the night, staring at Tom's truck. "Eddie's watching us."

Tom shrugs.

I swallow. "No one's ever asked me before, never asked me why I sing songs."

He arches an eyebrow. "Not even Dylan?"

I shake my head.

"Not even Emily?"

"It'd be like asking her why she takes so many pictures. It's just obvious I guess."

"Why *does* she take so many pictures?" Tom asks. He picks up my hand and clips a duct tape bracelet over my fingers. It glides across my skin and settles on my arm. Tom moves it with his finger, slowly circling it around.

It is hard to keep my voice normal. "She's afraid of losing people. She's afraid she'll forget things about them."

My words come out slow and heavy maybe because my heart is fighting with two strange things. It's tingling because Tom's touching me and it's aching sadness for Emmie and her sweetness.

Tom leans closer. "Some things you never forget though."

"I know." My voice becomes a whisper with a mind of its own.

"Some people either. Right, Commie?"

I don't get a chance to answer because my voice has succumbed to flip flops of Heaven because Tom's lips are pressing against mine. My voice is too close to the action to do anything but rejoice.

----o----

When we stop kissing I ask him, "Did you always know he was gay?"

Tom shrugs. "Not always."

He turns his head away.

"He used to like me," Tom says. "That's how I figured it out. Then he pretended like he didn't. That's when the whole pact thing happened."

I swallow hard. I take his hand in mine and ask him because I have to know. I hate to know now. "Did you ever like him back? That way?"

He turns back to me and squeezes my hand. "No."

Then everything inside me melts because he kisses me and my stomach molds into his and my hands press into his chest and his hair.

"I don't think I'm rebounding," I say when we stop. "Good."

- - - - o - - - -

After Tom walks me to the door, I don't go inside. Instead, I turn around to wave at him driving away. It feels like he's going away forever, like I'll never see him again. Eddie Caron's standing at the end of his driveway.

Tom's truck's headlights flash him into light. He scowls. His eyes glint yellow from the light's reflection.

"Hey, Eddie!" I yell.

He doesn't say anything, doesn't even lift up his hand to wave.

"Goodnight, Eddie!" I try again.

He still doesn't move. I shiver and open up the door, stepping into the warm light of my house and my mother's million trillion questions about Tom and if I'm moving too fast and if I'm happy.

"I want you to be happy, baby, just be careful. You don't want to jump into a new relationship too soon," she says, leaning against the kitchen counter.

"You don't like Tom?" I bristle.

"I like Tom very much. He's always been a special boy. Do you remember how he used to write you love notes in kindergarten?"

"No." I try to remember. I don't. "I thought that was Dylan."

"It was Tom." She smiles and opens up her arms for a hug. I step into them and all is good in the world, again, for both of us.

----o----

I call Em on her cell phone, which I know she keeps beside her bed for late-night friendship needs.

"I'm completely in lust with Tom," I whisper so my mom won't hear.

"I know."

"It's too soon," I say and slip my feet out of my bed. I pad over to the window, move the curtain to look down on the street where Dylan told me he was gay, to look down at the night sky.

"It's pretty soon," Em whispers back. She yawns.

"I woke you up."

"It's okay."

"He and Dylan got in a fight at the Y tonight."

"Oh my God."

"It was freaky," I said. "Like some sort of weird Neanderthal-caveman thing."

"They were fighting over you?"

I grab onto the curtain of the window a little tighter,

and look toward Eddie's house. "Yes. No. I don't know. It was weird. I really like Tom though."

A large shadow walks down Eddie Caron's driveway and then stands on the road, outside my house staring up at it. I can only make out the shadows of him. I don't move.

Em starts whispering again, "Sometimes things aren't logical. Sometimes things don't follow timetables, you know? If you like Tom, you like him. If he's a rebound, he's a rebound. At least you're not being a Mallory and wallowing in self-pity and playing the whole 'poor me I've got a gay ex-boyfriend' thing."

"Yeah." I lift my hand to wave to Eddie, because that's who it has to be out there.

He doesn't wave back. Maybe he can't see me. Instead, he lifts his head toward the sky. A plane's lights blink far above us. Its cabin is probably full of sleeping passengers ready to land in new places, start new adventures, maybe even new lives.

"Do you think he's a rebound?" I ask Em.

"No."

"Why not?" I ask her as Eddie turns and walks back to his house, a slow shuffle toward home in the night.

"Because I think you guys are meant to be. You've been lusting after each other since middle school, you've just been suppressing it."

I let that thought drift into me and lean my head against the cold window. "I just saw Eddie Caron outside, staring up at my house."

"Oh my God. That's freaky," Em forgets to whisper and it takes a second before I hear her mom's voice yell for her to get off the phone.

"Crap," Em says. "Gotta go. Sorry. Bye."

I hold my phone and watch Eddie enter his house. He goes through the door, doesn't turn a light on, and just steps inside. He must know his way through his house in the dark. Above us in the sky, the plane is gone. It's moved on.

BECAUSE MY MIND KEEPS FLASHING on images of Dylan's fist hitting Tom's face and because I am resisting the urge to not stare out the window at Eddie or to obsess about the fact that Dylan cheated on me with Mimi, the stupid stereotyped arch villainess of my life, I start another list on my computer.

Reasons Not to Have a Crush on Tom Tanner

1. It's a rebound thing and he is far too cute to be a rebound thing with those big soccer legs of his. Don't obsess about that!

2. Because he makes things out of duct tape and that's a little weird, although in a sort of kinky way it could be . . . Don't obsess about that either!

3. Because he obviously is a corruptive force on your morality because he makes you obsess about things that you shouldn't be obsessing about.

4. Because he makes you wonder why you shouldn't be thinking those obsessing thoughts about those things.

5. Because it is too soon. It is too soon and it would sully your post relationship with Dylan who was perfect, even if he was gay. Okay, that's not true, since he had a thing with Mimi Cote, which is too disgusting for words. This is turning out to not be a good reason. I should cross it out.

6. Because he makes you wonder if having sex with a straight guy is different than having sex with a gay guy. DO NOT THINK ABOUT THAT EITHER.

7. Because he knew Dylan had a fling with Mimi and didn't tell you.

8. Because he keeps eighth-grade promises even if no one else does.

```
E-------3-----3-------------3--------|
A--------3-------3----------3--------|
D------------0----0--------0---------|
G--------------0-----2---X-----------|
B---------------X-------0---3--------|
E------------------3-------X---------|
```

Thursday

"I THINK I HAVE A crush on Tom Tanner," I tell Emily the moment we're out of my driveway.

"Damn. That was fast," she says in a completely ironic way. "It's not like you told me that last night or anything."

"Shut up."

She whoops and slaps me on the leg. Then she starts grinning from ear to ear and I am too.

"I'm sure it's just a rebound thing," I say, still smiling.

"Of course. Is he a good kisser?"

She bites the end of her fingers.

I hit her hand away from her mouth. "No biting!"

She shakes her head at me.

"And he does make all those things with duct tape," I say and let my sentence dangle there.

Em wiggles her eyebrows. "Kinky."

Someone in a minivan honks at her because she's cut them off and she screams at them, "Hey! No honking! We don't honk at people in Maine!"

I check out their license. "They're from Connecticut."

"They should know better," she says, mad now. Then she forgets, races around the schoolhouse corner, and smiles. "You got over Dylan fast."

I gulp and watch the angry New Yorkers in front of us flail their arms around. "I know. I feel guilty."

"Don't. He got over you."

I shrug. I tell her the rest about the Y and about Mimi and Tom.

"Damn, you've had a week. Your voice is better today," she says after I'm done and turns on the radio.

"Yeah." I hadn't noticed, but it's perfect now. "Do you think it's bad that I got over Dylan so quick?"

"No!" She gives me big eyes. "I do not! You need to live, girl."

"Yeah," I say.

"Yeah!" she shouts it.

I shout it back. "Yeah!"

"You know, if you think about it, you and Tom were always meant to be together. He gave you that ILOVEU ring in first grade or something. Remember? And then Mimi borrowed it and you let her and then she lost it." Em turns onto another road.

I remember. Mimi's always wanted what's mine. Dylan's always wanted to be who he really is. Tom's always wanted me. And what have I always wanted?

We pass the blueberry barrens. There's a dusting of frost covering the boulders, the short bushes making it all more magical than barren, or maybe the barrenness is magical.

Em presses the CD button. "You want to sing?"

"Yeah."

We sing the cheesy musical music. Then Emily changes the CD. "That's Dylan music. That's not your music. Let's listen to some Dar Williams."

"Sing to folk stuff?" I say.

"Yeah. Sound good?"

The turned-up volume of guitars and Dar Williams's

sweet voice blares through her speakers. Em snaps a picture of me singing. I wish I had Gabriel, my guitar. I take out the little duct tape one in my purse and pretend to play it. Em laughs and takes another picture. She's so into it, she almost rear-ends the New York minivan. We just laugh and turn up the music.

"Yeah," I yell. "Sounds good."

Then we start to sing. My voice sounds low and full of things. My voice sounds like me, not a show-tune voice, but a folk voice, like there should be guitars playing with it. And the thing is, I like it. I like it. It's good.

DYLAN WAITS BY MY LONG metal locker, number 238 for anyone interested, and leans his body against it, just like he used to. I swallow. Maybe I imagined everything. Maybe it was all a big, rotten joke. But Dylan's shaking hands and sad dog eyes tell me it's true—all of it. All of it. My heart caves in, but my feet keep moving on automatic pilot.

"Hi," I say.

"Hi," he says and tilts his head just a little bit to the right. It's so sad that I reach out, pull him to me and hug him, while people walk around us. People turn and stare. People don't look on purpose, but everybody, everybody sees.

He lets go first and says, wiping at his eye with the back of his hand, "I read your note."

I nod.

His voice cracks. "Thanks. It meant a lot to me. You mean a lot to me."

"Yeah," I swipe at a tear that's escaped out his eye and follows the contours of his cheek, racing for his chin. "You mean a lot to me too."

He swallows big, nods, moves aside so I can put my stuff in my locker. He helps me pull off my coat. I hang it up, grab my things, try to figure out what to say. "You know Eddie Caron is threatening to beat you up?"

He shrugs. "He's always threatening to beat someone up."

"I wouldn't be talking about beating people up. You nailed Tom last night."

Dylan smiles. "Gay guys can hit too, you know."

"Thank you, Mr. Let's-Break-the-Stereotype."

Em walks by and mouths, "You okay?" I nod.

"You know, Eddie Caron used to be nice."

Dylan barks. "When was that?"

"When we were little," I say, remembering Eddie building castles in the dirt at the edge of the road, scaring off the third-grade school bus bullies on our first day of kindergarten.

Dylan shifts his weight back against a locker, looking more casual than he has all week, and Anna walks by giving us a thumbs-up sign like she's proud of us just for talking. We both give a little wave back and then Dylan says, "You're always trying to see the good in everybody, Belle. Sometimes there's no good to see."

I nod. The air between us is soft and hard, easy and difficult. I can taste the worry in it. "I heard you and Bob were going to the dance."

"Yeah." He shifts his weight on his feet, pushes a hand through that golden hair, my golden boy, my Dylan. "You okay with that?"

I step back. My eyes search his. My hands don't tingle. But my heart leaps with love.

"Yeah," I say because I am.

"Where's Gabriel?"

"I haven't been playing her," I pause and watch Em fumble around, probably looking for her camera. "Not since we broke up."

"That's stupid."

"I know." I smile and shrug because it is stupid, to

give up something that's important to me so easily. "Just call me stupid."

Then all of a sudden, Dylan smiles and he's back, all golden, all glowing, and says, "You're my best friend, Belle."

I scunch up my nose at him. He used to call that move the Belle Bunny Nose. "Yeah, you're mine, too. But I'm really pissed at you about the Mimi thing."

"That was stupid."

"Yeah, it was. You lied to me a lot you know, about Mimi, about Bob," I say, but the truth is it doesn't hurt at all right now, all those lies.

"You are a twerp," I tease and then I punch him in the shoulder. He punches me back. I punch him again, harder. He rubs his arm and says, "Can you help me with my economics homework sometime?"

I shake my head at him and smile. "You're such a user."

He laughs. "I know."

The his face turns serious. "I *was* attracted to you, you know."

I smile. "I know."

"You know . . . in the sexual way."

I nod, and feel my cheeks flame red. "But you were gay."

He nods. "I think I made myself not gay somehow, but it wasn't real. I mean . . . I don't mean that you aren't attractive."

He laughs.

"But I like guys better," he finishes. He looks up toward the ceiling like he wants to hide in the water stains.

His eyes shift back down to me. He bites his lip and he smiles.

"You like boys *a lot* better," I say and he nods and grabs me into a hug.

I let him. I hug him back and it feels good, not tingling good, but good. But what feels the best is how I no longer hurt.

"I'm not sure Bob is good enough for you," I say.

He glares at me. "And what about Tom? Like he's good enough?"

I bite my lip. The bell rings. "Maybe we shouldn't go there, Slugger."

He hustles me off away from the lockers and down the hall, like he used to when we were going out, only it feels like a friend kind of hustle, like Emily. "Probably."

EM TAKES A PICTURE OF us, smiling at each other like two trees in the middle of summer, sharing the secret of the wind. Then she runs off to find Shawn.

AFTER DYLAN'S SCOOTED INTO ECONOMICS and I'm walking to law class I hear it again, the nasty whisper hate of it, bouncing past Kara Raymond's shoulders and latching itself to me.

"Fag hag."

I whirl around and see her. Mimi. The girl Dylan didn't choose when he chose me. Or maybe he did. What do I know? I stomp over to her. She's frozen there with her little miniskirt stretched across the bottom circles of her round body. She's frozen there, staring, staring, staring at me out of her too-much-eye-shadow eyes and her sad hair. She's frozen there, staring, staring, staring with hate smashing out of her pores, out of her clothes, out of her hair.

I stop two inches from her. My hands ball into fists. Sebastian Puller, an evil junior boy who is always getting suspended, yells, "Cat fight."

Mimi would step back, I know, but she's frozen. She smells like her mother's cigarettes. Her mother smokes. Whenever I went over to play, I'd smell like it, too.

"Mimi," I say. "You need to get a life."

Her eyes squint at me. But she does it again. She says it again, spits it out.

"Fag hag."

Everyone in the circle around us pulls in their breaths, but I breathe out and laugh. I laugh because it's too stupid, so stupid really. Kara Raymond giggles too and then turns self-righteous and is a second away from ripping into Mimi, but I beat her to it.

"What, Mimi? I'm a fag hag because I used to go out with Dylan, who you, obviously, are still in love with? I'm a fag hag because I don't care if someone's gay, I'm still friends with him. Is that what's wrong? What? Should I be dragging him behind a pickup truck or dropping him off a bridge? Is that what you think? Jesus. Dylan's a way better person than you'll ever be, Mimi. And he's my friend. Yeah, my friend and if that makes me a goddamn fag hag then I don't give a shit!"

The second bell rings. The late bell. Then Mimi spits it out at me, "You're so fucking deluded, Belle. You think everybody's all good all the time, but they aren't. You make everybody into song lyrics and heroes, but nobody's good. Nobody is."

"Shut up, Mimi. Don't be such a bitch!" Kara Raymond yells, trying to come to my rescue, but I don't need a rescue, I don't think.

"That's crap," I say.

She arches an eyebrow. "Oh, right? Like your little gay boyfriend wasn't all a big fake. Did you know he kissed me right when you guys first started going out? Did you know that?"

I sigh out my words, "Yeah, I know that."

She pauses for a second and then she starts in again. "And I bet you think Tom's a handsome prince too, huh? Well, he's not. He's a sucky kisser. Not like you'll ever know that, because you only like gay boys, right? He's liked you for fucking ever and you never even looked his way, not until Dylan dumped you."

My hand shakes. Kara starts charging at Mimi again but I hold her back. "Shut up, Mimi."

"Why? Because you don't want to hear about how delusional you are?"

I let go of Kara and she surges forward with her warrior voice, "Shut the hell up, Mimi, like you and your push-up bras aren't delusional? Belle is . . ."

But I don't hear her because I've whirled around and am walking away. I'm walking away to my law class and I don't care. I don't care about Mimi Cote or evil Sebastian Puller or vigilant Kara Raymond or all the people watching. I don't care about being a fag hag or delusional or that I just swore in the middle of school and if a teacher finds out I'll get the first detention in my life. I don't care about anything except trying to make the staccato beat of my heart slow down.

"Dyke!"

I whirl around and there's Mimi Cote still standing in the middle of the hallway, her middle finger sticking up at me.

Kara starts laughing. "Dyke? Is that all you can come up with Mimi? Jesus, Belle's the most pathetically hetero girl in the school. She's gone from Dylan to Tom in like two days or something. God."

"Four days," I shout down the hall smiling. "Four days if you count Saturday. Three if you don't."

She stares at me and then I add, "And he is too a good kisser. He's a phenomenal kisser!"

Shawn has come down the hall and is standing beside me and he lets out a big cowboy YEEHAW! Then he starts clapping. Kara claps too and some other people join in. Nobody's even pretending to hurry off to class because the Mimi-Belle showdown is too worthy, like having reality TV in the hallway, I guess.

"You're a slut then," Mimi spits out, but it's too late to mean anything. She's too far gone.

Shawn slaps me five. I kind of miss his hand because I am not the best high-five hand slapper, but it's still good.

And then I laugh too, because it's so sad really. I laugh because Kara is so right and it's ridiculous how hormone-ruled I am. I laugh because Mimi is such a pathetic villain, unoriginal, boring. And the crazy thing is back in eighth grade when we were cheerleaders that stuff she said would have torn me apart. My world would have ended right there.

Now?

Now I've got a gay ex-boyfriend, a rebound relationship, and a semi-psycho next-door neighbor who watches my bedroom window at night.

But I will not be a Mallory about this. I will just move on. I mean, once I get home and pick up Gabriel, I could probably write a really good song about all of this. That happy little thought makes me bebop down the hallway, happier than I have any right to be.

At lunch, Emily and I abandon our normal table and sit with the soccer boys. Tom sits across from me and stretches his legs out. He watches me drink my Postum and chomps into his pizza slice.

"Heard you had a little spat with Mimi Cote." He raises one eyebrow. How does he do that?

"Yeah."

I put my mug up to my mouth so I don't have to talk about it, but Emily, who has been telling Shawn all about the outfit she's wearing to the dance, stops mid-sentence and barks, "What?"

"Mimi's been calling me a fag hag," I explain. "So, I told her to stop."

Emily's nostrils flare the way my mom's do when she's mad. "That bitch! I'll kill her."

Shawn starts laughing and clamps his hand over Emily's mouth. "Calm down, mighty one. Belle's got it under control, don't you, Belle?"

"Yeah," I answer. Tom smiles at me and shakes his head. "I've got it under control."

End of conversation, right? Wrong.

"She called you a dyke, too. Right?" Tom says. A slow smile creeps across his face. I glare at him, because we both know he's just trying to get Em riled up, which the whole town knows doesn't take much.

Emily licks Shawn's hand to get him to move it. He does, completely grossed out, and wipes it on his thigh.

Emily pays no attention, she's too busy yelling, "She did what?"

I sip my Postum. "She called me a dyke."

Emily rants for a minute, while the rest of us laugh at her. She finally catches on. "What? What? Don't you even care?"

I shake my head. "Nope. It's sad. She's sad, really."

Emily shakes her head. "Well, I think she's a bitch."

"A sad bitch," I agree.

"You're not, are you?" Shawn asks me, eyes twinkling.

"What?"

"Gay?"

Emily throws down her bagel. "Jesus! How stupid are you?"

She leaps up from the table and stomps off toward the lunch line. Shawn smiles and saunters after her. Tom and I watch them argue. Em keeps pointing at him. Shawn keeps opening his arms up like he's surrendering or expecting a hug, only he keeps stepping backwards.

"They're already fighting," I say. "They're barely going out."

"Must be love," Tom says.

He holds up his pizza slice. "Want some?"

I shake my head.

"So are you?" He raises that eyebrow again.

I kick him under the table and he grabs my foot between his metal-strong calves, keeps it there. My cheeks flame. My leg feels like it's on fire, but it's a good, good fire. I glare at him.

"Nope," he smiles. "I'd say not."

He keeps my foot there for all of lunch. I pretend like I want to get away, but I don't. I don't want to at all.

Our fetal pig's flesh bears the marks of knives and invasions. Em snaps a picture.

"God, she's gross," she says.

"She's sad, really," I say, trying to move some skin around to make her look whole again, but the truth is, she never will be. "What do they do with them, when we're done?"

Em shrugs. Her lip quivers. "Throw them away?"

"I don't want them to throw Pamela away in some dumpster somewhere," I say.

"I want to remember her."

Em nods, shows me her camera. "That's why I took the pictures. I'll download them and give you one, okay?"

Em took a lot of pictures of Dylan and me. Someday I'll look at them again, and try to figure everything out, but not now, not yet. Pamela the Fetal Pig? Her picture I can handle.

I smile at her, my Emily friend, and I nod. "Yeah, I'd like that. You and Shawn okay?"

She turns the camera at herself and snaps away. "Yeah. But sometimes he's so dumb. He's lucky he's cute."

She puts the camera down. Mr. Zeki's gabbing to the cute student teacher in the front of the class and paying no attention to us. Em says, "What should we do about Mimi?"

"Mimi? Nothing."

Em does not like this answer. She drums her fingers against the lab table and waits.

"We could name our next fetal pig after her?"

Em stares down at the pathetic Pamela. "That is a damn good idea."

IN GERMAN, TOM RAISES HIS eyebrows at me when I come into class. I blush and yank out my textbook, which we never use. The trees outside have lost all their leaves now. It's gray and claustrophobic out there. Another Maine almost-winter day.

Tom clears his throat behind me.

I turn around.

"Aren't you going to say, 'Hi'?" he asks. He smiles.

My heart leaps against my ribs, but I act cool. I will not show it. "Hi."

His smile widens. I blush. He laughs.

Crash yells out, "Tom and Belle are flirting again."

Herr Reitz adjusts his clown nose. It's hard to take a teacher seriously when they have a multi-colored wig stuck on their head and giant banana shoes, but he puts on a serious voice. "Can you say it in German, Rasheesh?"

Crash shakes his head. "Hell, no."

Then he holds up his hands and says, "Tomen and Bellen ist geflirten, ja?"

He bows. Herr Reitz glares at him. He honks his clown nose. "Belle, why don't you escape these idiots and bring this note to the office for me, bitte?"

I take the note. Herr Reitz nods and smiles. When I walk by Tom's desk, my blush deepens, heating my cheeks the way it always does. Tom winks and inside my chest, my heart starts singing songs.

THEN IT HAPPENS.

I'm alone in the hallway, running the errand for Herr Reitz, thinking about how going to the dance might not be that big a deal at all if I get to dance with Tom. It's when I'm imagining Tom's hand pressed into the bottom of my back that Eddie Caron steps out from the boys' bathroom. I smile at him, but my ancient protector does not smile back. What was it Mimi said? That I was delusional, always expecting the best from people, even people who stand outside on the road and stare up at my room at night.

"Eddie?" my voice squeaks.

He moves in front of me, blocking my way back to class. The radiator next to me hisses and clicks like it's getting ready to explode.

I move to the left. He moves to the left. I move to the right. He moves to the right.

"Eddie, let me get by," I say, trying to make my voice strong. The radiator clicks louder. Eddie's eyes stare me down like a dog stares you down when it's deciding whether to obey your command or not.

He's huge. His black t-shirt stretches over a chest that's much too wide to be consider human sized. It's more tractor-trailer size. When we were little, he used to pull toy tractor trailers down the street and put ants inside. He'd say he was taking them to better weather in Florida. I stare at him, this massive man, this not-moving Eddie, and wonder where that little boy went.

The radiator finally clanks on, a big growl and hiss, all combined. No one is in the hall to hear it except us.

Eddie moves. He grabs my arm in his fleshy fingers. I force myself not to panic. We are in the hall. This is Eddie Caron, my neighbor. He's not mad at me. He's mad at Dylan. We are in school. I am safe. "Let me go, Eddie!"

He glares. Fingers tighten.

"So gay-boy Dylan dumped you, huh? And bing—you go out with Tom Tanner. Tom Tanner, a freaking soccer punk?"

"He's not a soccer punk," I say and forget to be scared.

Eddie isn't scared either. His fingers hurt my arm and his eyes look like Muffin's when she can't decide to scratch at you because she's so upset you've moved her off her law text book. "When's my turn, Belle? Huh, when the fuck is my turn?"

His other hand reaches up, grabs my other arm. His eyes jitter back and forth and his breath smells like beer.

"Jesus, Eddie! Are you drunk? What are you doing?" I twist like they said to do in that self-defense class Em and I took with Janine at the Y but my arms do not get free. Damn Janine. I step back. My arms stay in Eddie's hands. Fear pumps my blood to my skin. I wrench away, but my arms stay. "Eddie, let me go."

But this man who is the new Eddie doesn't listen. He doesn't listen. His steel fingers wrap around my arms tighter. I shake. My legs warp into plastic things and I kick at him, but he moves so my foot barely makes contact with his body. His eyes anger. He smashes me against the lockers. My head bashes against the back of one and throbs.

"Don't fight me," he grunt-talks real low, his face all close to mine. "Don't fight me, bitch."

"I'm not a bitch. I'm Belle, your goddamn neighbor. Eddie. Jesus," I spit out at him. "You're hurting me."

His eyes turn to hurt stars, airplanes flying away and never coming back. His eyes ache but his hands don't let go.

"And now, what, you doing super-soccer-star Tommy? What about me, Belle? What about me?" He shifts his arm up against my neck, the hard muscle of it squeezes my throat shut. I can't breathe. I can't speak. His other hand grabs at my breast and squeezes hard. Pain splinters off into my shoulder and heart. He snarls. "Too much for the gay boy to handle, huh? You know, he used to like me, Dylan did, when we were what, seven? Didn't know it then, though. I only just figured it out. Slow, stupid, Eddie right? You were slow too though, huh? Little Miss National Honor Society was pretty freaking slow too."

I lift my knee, but miss his groin, get only his thigh, but it's enough. It's enough to make him loosen and gasp. I shove at him, my old playmate, my old knight. I duck and slide away, racing, racing, down the hall. I round the corner and slam into Mimi Cote. She falls down and I reach my hand to help her up, but she jumps up herself and hisses at me, "Bitch."

Fag hag.
Slut.
Dyke.
Bitch.
Fag hag.
Dyke.
Slut.
Bitch.
I am none of these things.
I am none of these things.
None.

I AM A RUNNING GIRL. I run. I run. I run through the fluo-rescent-light halls and slam into the classroom. My face is almost crying. My hands shake. My heart beats hard, beats hard, too hard.

Everyone stares. Everyone. Tom's face blanks like a mannequin, but his eyes stare too, horrified, dark.

Herr Reitz grabs my jerking hand in his sweaty one. And I know what's going to happen and that I don't have much time. I plead with Herr Reitz, without words, with just eyes.

His voice is a question. "Belle?"

Tom leaps up. His mouth moves. "She's going to have a seizure."

He pulls me onto the floor. His eyes are large and brown, tree-bark good and scared.

FREAK.

That's what everyone will say about me now; what everyone will call me. Not fag hag, but freak.

Freak.

EMILY DRIVES ME HOME.

"I'm not supposed to have them."

"Did you have any caffeine?"

"No."

"Chew any gum?"

"No. Well, the other day, but it was the non-aspartame kind."

I stare out the car window but see nothing, just blurs. I can't focus. "I hit my head on the locker when he . . ."

I do not finish.

"Maybe that's it," Emily says. She takes a big breath. "Maybe it's the stress. You've been under a lot of stress."

My voice numbs the car. "Yeah."

Emily drives. "The nurse's office smells like puke."

"Yeah."

"He's suspended, you know. They suspended him," she says, anger tightening her voice. "They might expel him. Shawn saw him and said he was sobbing in the parking lot, just bawling his eyes out, saying, 'Tell Belle I'm sorry. Tell her I'm sorry.'"

I nod and pull Tom's soccer coat around me, trying to hide. I don't know where the coat came from, but I'm glad it's there. It smells like him. "Good."

"Tom said he put that under your head when you had your seizure," Emily sniffs in. "Dylan's gone ballistic. He was in the principal's office demanding to see you, saying he was going to sue the school if they didn't kick Eddie out. His hair was flopping all over the place. He still loves you, you know."

"He's gay."

"He's a good friend." Emily stops at a red light. There's a dog in the car next to us. Even though it's cold, the owner's got the window rolled down and the dog's snuffing up all the air, smiling at the cars.

"I wish I were a dog," I say.

"Dogs have seizures too."

"Great."

Emily touches my shoulder and I look at her. Kindness fills her eyes.

"Everyone will think I'm a freak." My voice breaks when I say it. I bite my lip and a gulp lodges itself in the middle of my throat, threatening to explode. I think, maybe it's not a gulp, but my heart, my heart looking for a place to escape.

Emily shrugs. "We'll spin it. We'll say Eddie gave you a concussion."

I shake my head. "Tom knows that's not it. Shawn too. I passed out Monday, remember. The whole freaking soccer team saw me."

The light turns green. Emily puts her hand back on the steering wheel.

"Sweetie, we will spin this. It will be fine. Tom doesn't care if you have seizures."

"You don't know that. You can't know that."

Emily says nothing for a minute and then she says in a soft mother voice, "God, Belle, you really like him."

"Yeah, I do."

I put the window down. Cold air rushes in and I hang my head out, a dog sniffing the air. It doesn't work, though. It doesn't make me smile.

My mother wants me to stay home from school tomorrow. The doctor confirms Emily's guess. Stress may have caused the seizure, or the head bash against the locker, or the momentary lack of oxygen. The emergency room says it's just a minor concussion.

"Just a minor concussion," my mother complains on the ride home. "Since when is a concussion minor?"

She puts me in bed. The phone rings and rings. The doorbell sounds. I do not move. I turn my head so that I can see Gabriel, my blue guitar, against the wall. I will have to tune her. I haven't played her for almost a week. She must be sad, not even going to school with me anymore. I used to skip lunch sometimes and play in the band room, or upstairs at German. Sometimes Em and Dylan and some other people like Anna or Kara would come and hang and listen. Poor Gabriel, no one is listening to her sing anymore. She's just an empty hole with no vibrations. My fingers twitch, but I can't pick her up.

My little duct tape guitar sits on the night table by my bed. I touch it with my finger and think about Tom. My heart flops upside down. The last thing I remember are his scared eyes.

"I don't know, she's got a concussion," my mom says to someone. Emily? Tom? No, my heart knows who it is. Somehow, I know it is Dylan.

He murmurs something to my mother and a minute later he opens my door, steps into my bedroom, sits on the edge of my bed. We used to call it our love bed.

His hand pushes hair from my forehead. His fingers brush tears from my cheek. "Sweetie."

I close my eyes. Why is everyone calling me sweetie lately?

"Belle?"

My eyes open again. Dylan leans closer and whispers, "I am so sorry."

My lip trembles. My arms open. He holds me to him. "Me too."

From across the room, by the window, Gabriel makes the sweet sound of a G chord, all by itself, like magic. Dylan doesn't even look up, just keeps his head next to mine, murmuring things I can't quite hear, but it sounds sweet and smooth and lilting like a lullaby.

He is so warm against me. He is so warm my shaking stops. My words come out solid, whole, plump like blueberries in August. "I love you."

He kisses my hair and he doesn't hesitate. He just says it right back, "I love you, too."

And I know we both mean it. And I know we don't need to say it for it to be true, but it's still nice to hear. And I know it's not the kind of love we both thought it was once, but that doesn't make it any less good or any less true.

He starts to sing, softly, an old Van Morrison song about beautiful, magical places and people being forever friends. It's not one of Dylan's opera songs, or one of my girl folk songs, but it is our song, our friendship song. His lullaby voice pushes me toward sleep, but before I shut my eyes, I notice Gabriel, my blue guitar, leaning against the wall. Tomorrow I will stand her up. Tomorrow I will buy new strings and play something good and sweet and in tune. And maybe I will buy some duct tape and make little people who will always be friends and I will stick them onto Em's dashboard and I will give one to Dylan and another one to Tom.

But that is for tomorrow.

For today, Dylan and I will fall asleep there on my love bed, lengthened out next to each other. We will hold each other throughout the night, the way we've always promised to, the way friends are supposed to when things go bad. Together, we will hold each other safe.

----o----

But this is no fairy tale and the Harvest King and Queen do not get to sleep together happily ever after throughout the night. Dylan is not suddenly ungay and I am not suddenly un-in-lust with Tom.

Everything is not suddenly better.

My mom does not even let him stay the night, of course. She lets him stay two hours and then hustles him away. He looks embarrassed that he's been in my bed and my mom's caught him, which is ridiculous because this is the first time he's been in my bed fully clothed and where nothing's happened.

I am groggy and tired but I wave goodbye.

After she lets him out, my mom comes and sits beside me, holding my hand.

"I want to go to school tomorrow," I tell her.

"We'll see."

"I'm going."

"We'll see."

I swallow and squeeze her hand. "I can't hide forever."

"You have a concussion, sweetie."

"I have to go to school," I say. "If I don't go tomorrow I'll never be brave enough to go back."

She kisses my forehead. "We'll see."

She starts humming a lullaby song, "Go to sleep, little whirl, close your pretense, blue skies."

I squeeze her hand and ask her. "Mom, do you mess up the words on purpose?"

She waits a second. She waits another one and sighs out, "Yes."

"Why do you do that?" I sit up straight and she gently puts her hands on my shoulders to push me back down.

She tucks the covers around me again and says, "Sometimes it's good to give people something they're not expecting. You get what I mean?"

I shake my head.

"Plus, it makes people laugh."

```
E-------3-----3-------------------3----------|
A-------3-------3-----------------3----------|
D---------------0------------------0---------|
G---------------0-----------2------x---------|
B------------------------X--------0----3-----|
E-----------------------------3-------X------|
```

Friday

THE OVERCAST SUNLIGHT SHIFTS THROUGH my windows and wakes me up. I stay there in my bed, and pull my pillow over my head. It's cool against my forehead. The memory of yesterday smacks itself back into my soul, like a sucker punch to the belly. And I jump up.

My hands do not jerk.

My head aches but does not spin.

I shoot a glance at the clock. It's ten o'clock, my mother didn't wake me up. I sigh, but can't be mad. Gabriel rests against the wall and I pick her up and imagine strumming a shuffling blues rhythm; strumming an E-chord down and up, down and up. But I just can't do it. Instead, I run my fingertips softly along the edge of her fret board.

My mom comes and leans against the door frame, arms crossed in front of her chest, smiling. "You going to play her soon?"

"Yep."

"Good."

----o----

We compromise. My mom had me sleep late and then lets me go to school late. I'm not happy about it, but it works.

Dropping me off, she hands me my gig case and her eyes go worried. "Stay safe, sweetie."

I nod and act all brave. "Don't worry. All's good."

Then I exit the car. The cold blasts me, whips through Tom's jacket and my shirt. My hair lashes out behind me, but I fight against the frigid wind and the muted cloudy sky and I walk forward into school.

----o----

The first person I see is Bob. He glares at me.

"Hey," I say and raise my hand to wave, but he just scurries through the empty corridor, feet slapping on the dirty linoleum, like I don't exist.

Then the bell for the period rings. I get there in time for lunch, but despite all my brave talk, I don't go. Instead, I walk through the halls, as everyone rushes out of their classes. I pass by Kara.

"Belle?" Her eyes wide. "You okay? I heard about . . ."

I cut her off, but smile. "I'm good."

She stares at me and nods and it's like there's a computer processor stuck behind her eyes, computing all sorts of information. "You going to lunch?"

I shake my head. "Nah."

I lift up Gabriel in my gig bag and say, "I'm going to study hall and play. Tell Em if you see her, okay?"

"Okay," Kara nods really emphatically like I've just told her the secret to stopping illegal detention of potential political insurgents' wives and children.

I pretty much ignore the other people I see, Andrew, Anna, Shawn, and just book it into the study hall room, pull out Gabriel in all her shiny blue glory, and then I begin to think about playing, but I don't. I just hold her in the position.

----o----

I sit in silence for a long time, just holding my guitar. It belonged to my dad once, this guitar. So, I sit there and imagine him playing it, but it isn't real. It's just silence. Nothing.

I close my eyes.

----o----

The sound of a pair of slow, loud clapping hands breaks me out of it.

Tom sits on top of a desk by the door. I'm in the middle of the room, Gabriel on my lap and my eyes are closed and I'm not even playing her. I bite my lip and look away, worried that he'll think of me as the freak seizure girl.

I clear my throat. "Do you want your jacket back?"

"What?" Tom stands up and starts toward me. I fiddle with the strings, pretending like I'm tuning them.

"I said, 'Do you want your coat back?'"

"You said, 'jacket,'" he says, standing just a foot away from me.

"Whatever." My heart beats too fast, ready for the pain. "Do you want it?"

I balance Gabriel on a nearby desk and start pulling my arms out of Tom's jacket. I feel like I've lost another layer of myself, like I'm part naked without it. I hold it out to him.

"I don't want my jacket, Belle." He shakes his head like I've failed him, which I guess I have. "Are you okay?"

"Yeah," I nod and shrug. Then I pull the jacket back to me and clutch it against my chest.

"Dylan told me he went to your house last night," Tom says, leaning back against a desk and crossing his arms in front of him. "He said you were doing okay, that Eddie didn't hurt you too much."

"Yeah." I look away. I look back. I don't know where to look. I decide to focus on my Snoopy shoes. Good ole Snoopy, clutching those balloons, hoping to fly away.

Tom touches my arm and I jump. He stares into my eyes, forcing me to look, seeming startled himself, but serious, really serious. "Do you still love him?"

I tilt my head. "What?"

"You heard me. Don't make me say it again," he says, pleading now, but steady, strong.

"Of course, I love him," I say. "I'll always love him, but I don't love him love him like in a sexual romantic way. Does that make sense?"

He nods and turns, paces away a few steps, runs his hand through his hair. That place in his cheek spasms. He looks up in the air and then back at me. "It just about killed me when he said he slept with you."

"He didn't sleep with me! He hugged me!" I yell and I toss Tom's jacket onto a desk, angry and stomp closer to him. The light above our heads buzzes and flickers out. "That's not the same thing."

He lifts an eyebrow. "It isn't?"

"You know it isn't."

He pauses and says slowly like every word matters,

"How would you feel if you found out I was on a bed hugging Mimi Cote for hours?"

It is so quiet I can hear the clock on the wall tick away the seconds as my heart breaks. "Fully clothed?"

He nods. "Fully clothed."

"I'd tear her heart out."

He smiles, but it's just a little, sad smile and my heart, my own heart flip flops in my chest and aches for him. I swallow hard. "I'm so sorry. He came and I was so sad, but nothing happened. I'm sorry."

I bite my lip and the words come out before I can stop them. "I wish it was you. I wish it was you holding me."

He scratches at his hair and then holds open his arms, and I don't think. I rush into them.

"I'm sorry," I say. "I'm sorry."

And he leans in and kisses me, so much harder, so much deeper than our other two kisses. It's long and full of comforter cover dreams and bathtubs and singing on grassy lawns holding hands and it's full of want and need and love.

I sigh against him. I lean against him and he leans against me. Our hands hold each other up and our lips talk and talk and tell each other's soul secrets, all without words.

----o----

His hands rub my back in little circles as we leave the study hall and head to class and I manage to say, "What about the seizure thing?"

"What about it?" Tom asks. He holds the door.

"Well, I have seizures, you know. I mean, people are

probably going to think I'm a freak and everything and if you hang out with me . . ."

Tom puts a finger over my lips. "Belle, I knew you had seizures."

"You did?" my voice squeaks and my lips touch his finger as they move. My free hand grabs at his shirt, holds the cotton in between my fingers.

"Belle, I hate to tell you this, but this is Eastbrook. Everybody knows you have seizures."

I let go of his shirt, turn my head up to him. "They do?"

He laughs and pulls me along with him down the hallway. "Commie, the People, they know everything."

---- o ----

Mr. Zeki checks me out when I go into class. Tom plants a kiss on my cheek and heads off. Mr. Zeki wiggles his eyebrows at me and Em groans, "Dirty old man."

Mr. Zeki heads to our table and squats down beside me. "You doing okay, Belle? Feeling alright?"

I nod.

He eyes me like I'm lying and says in his super-effeminate voice, "I'd like to crush that Eddie Caron boy."

He hits his fist into his palm and it's all I can do not to laugh. Em snorts next to me. Mr. Zeki doesn't notice. Instead, he puts his hand on my shoulder. "Let me know if there's anything I can do for you."

He nods at Em. "For either of you girls."

"Um, thanks," I say and look to Em for help. She just gives me big eyes and Mr. Zeki sashays away and announces,

"I'm tired. It's Friday. How about you all talk and pretend to study for the test Monday? I'm going to sit here, take some Motrin, and do a crossword."

"Looks like you just got yourself a bodyguard," Anna says to me. Then she smiles. "Two if you want me."

I smile back. "I'll be okay."

----o----

After we assure all the curious around us that Eddie did not rape me and I am fine and will be going to the dance with Tom, Em and I get down to our serious talk.

"Bob and Dylan had a huge fight in the cafeteria before school," she says, pulling out a piece of gum and munching on it. "It was really embarrassing. Bob just flew into Dylan about what happened last night."

"What happened last night?" I ask her, pulling out my Tic Tacs. "Is my breath bad?"

"No, it's fine," she says, pointing at her gum. "That was not a sign. I have bad breath. I had coffee at lunch since you weren't there."

"You never drink coffee," I say, confused and popping in some Tic Tacs anyway.

"That's because I know you can't."

"You still chew gum. I can't have that either, unless it's the crappy kind."

She smiles. "Friendship can only go so far."

I whack her with my notebook, but not hard. She whacks me back and I pretend to be all smiley happy, but what I'm really thinking is that I don't know who anyone is, really, not even Emily, my best friend. I whack her again.

"Girls!" Mr. Zeki yells. "Isn't Miss Philbrick recovering from a head injury?"

"Sorry!" Em yells. "I won't hurt her."

She giggles behind her hand and adds, "Much."

Mr. Zeki shakes his head and goes back to his crossword. Anna turns around and hisses, "He is so in love with you two."

"We get our brownie points where we can," Em says.

I lower my voice once Anna turns around. "So, what happened last night?"

Em shoots me a look that means she thinks I'm being stupid on purpose.

"What?" I say.

"About you guys sleeping together."

"We did not sleep together!" I yell.

Everyone turns around and starts laughing. Mr. Zeki shouts, "Good to know! If you do, use a condom! We all had our little safe-sex lecture when we were freshman. Don't make me have to give it again."

I flush so much my face burns. Em doubles over laughing. When she's done, I tell her what happened. She shakes her head when I'm done. "That's not how Bob made it sound."

"Bob's an idiot," I say.

She agrees, snaps her gum. "Dylan can do better."

"Do you think they'll make up and go to the dance tonight?" I ask her.

"Probably," she shrugs, puts her notebook back in her bag. "Are you still going with Tom?"

I smile, which she understands as a yes.

"He was pretty pissed when he heard about you and Dylan last night," she says. "Did you guys talk about it?"

"Yeah," I say, remembering his lips on my lips, his hands on my back, that electric feeling. I start blushing again. "We talked. Did you send him to hear me play?"

"Yeah. He really likes you, you know."

"I really like him."

"Good," she nods at my gig bag, safe over by the lab sinks, tucked out of the way. "I'm glad you're playing again."

I tuck my arm into hers and she leans her head on my shoulder when I say, "I didn't actually play yet."

"God, don't tell me you just sat there."

"Fine. I won't tell you."

She shakes her head. "I don't know what I'm going to do with you."

"Love me?" I suggest.

She shrugs. "That works."

----o----

The hardest part of the day is going to German, because that's where it all happened, where everybody saw me jerk and shake and pass out.

Tom told me it didn't last long, maybe five seconds, but that doesn't make me feel better.

Anna walks with me because she has Spanish next door. "You okay?"

"Yeah," I say, but truth is I'm close to hyperventilating as I walk by the radiator where it happened. Truth is, I'd rather do anything than tromp through that door and go into German.

Anna slaps me on the back. "Go get 'em, tiger."

----o----

One step over the threshold. Another step into the room. I stare at the floor, at the cracked tiles. No, that's no good. I look up, straight ahead.

Herr Reitz opens his arms up wide and says, "Belle, guten tag!"

He is trying too hard. He snaps the straps on his lederhosen and smiles too big.

I look out the window at the sky. It's actually blue right now. The tree branches poke into it, scraping against it. My heart skitters to the side. "Guten tag."

As quickly as possible, I file into the room. Tom barrels in after me, slams into his seat, and reaches out to touch my shoulder.

"Hey, hot stuff," he whispers.

"Hot stuff?"

Crash starts laughing and says like everything's normal, "Herr Reitz, Tomen and Bellen is geflirten again."

"Rasheesh! Will you at least try to say it in German," Herr Reitz scolds and starts writing out how to say it on the board. Everybody laughs. Tom especially. I can't believe it. It's like everything is fine.

But it isn't. Of course it isn't. Bob coughs and raises

his hand and says, "Herr Reitz, I'm no longer comfortable sitting near Belle. I'd like to move."

My heart falls onto the floor. Tears rush to my eyes, but hate comes faster, quicker. Tom stands up behind me. Herr Reitz's arm freezes in the middle of a word. And Bob, Bob just keeps standing there in his jeans that ride up his butt too high and his white ankles sticking out. Dylan left me for him, for him.

Herr Reitz turns around, nods at Tom. "Sit down, Tom."

Tom sits and reaches his leg forward to hook his foot around my foot beneath my chair. A tiny red spider crawls across the corner of my desk. He's so small, like I'd like to be, scurrying around with nobody noticing him.

Herr Reitz stares at Bob. His cheeks bulge out and in, out and in, just like my heart. He takes a breath and says, "Bob. You want to move?"

Bob nods. The spider scampers off the top of my desk and hides on the side.

"Your seat?"

"Yes, my seat." Bob's voice is the strongest I've ever heard it.

Herr Reitz crosses his arms in front of his lederhosen. "Because of Belle?"

Bob shifts his weight. His eyes glance at me. My hands tremble, not in a seizure way, but in an angry, hate, scared way. Tom's foot tugs against mine. The spider drops onto my leg and is still, waiting.

"Yeah," Bob says, "because of Belle."

Hate frames his words.

Herr Reitz nods really slowly and as if he's a reporter trying to get the facts straight he says, "Because of what happened in class yesterday?"

Bob nods back, just as slowly.

"I thought so," Herr Reitz says and he straightens up, sighs. "Okay, Bob, you can move. You can move right out that door."

Bob's body is still. The rest of us gasp but don't say anything, not even Crash. Then Bob comes to life, his voice high and scared, and Bob-like. "What do you mean? *I* have to leave? She's the freak!"

Tom jumps up and lunges toward Bob, but little Crash gets in the way. At the same time, Herr Reitz strides down between the desks so he's right in front of Bob. "Out. Just get out! I'm ashamed to be your teacher."

Bob sputters. Tom relaxes enough so that he doesn't look as if he's going to immediately tear out Bob's throat, but not by much. I sink into my chair and cover my eyes with my hands.

"What do you think, Bob?" Herr Reitz says. "Are you going to leave yourself or am I going to have to have Tom escort you?"

Bob's eyes start watering and I feel bad. I lift up my head and reach out my hand. "Bob."

But he just grabs his books and runs right by me, out into the hall, and away.

My hand still reaches out to the air. Crash slaps it five because somebody has to do something, I guess. Herr Reitz comes and kneels in front of me. His bologna halitosis breath hits me full force. "Belle? You okay? You want to leave?"

"No." I shake my head. I look into Crash's eyes, Tom's. "I want to stay."

----o----

"I'll pick you up for the dance?" Tom says when the bell rings. He doesn't ask me if I'm okay about the whole Bob scene, which is good, because it would probably push me over the edge and into the land of melodrama girl, where nothing can stop the tears or the screaming or me from finding Bob's pasty butt and kicking it into New Hampshire.

"Sure," I say and smile up at him. I zip Gabriel back into her gig bag.

Tom shakes his head at me, while I pull Gabriel's bag over my shoulder. "How did I get so lucky?"

"You?" I am stunned.

"Yeah, me." There goes that Tom smile again, straight to my heart. I shake my head, because this is all so strange and raw and new and good, like your leg right after you shave it. I think about all those years of high school with Tom calling me a Commie and me cringing whenever he was around because I used to like him in middle school and he so obviously was this jock boy whose deepest emotion was teasing. Not that teasing is an emotion, but that's how shallow I thought he was.

"I can't believe you," I tell Tom.

"What do you mean?" He moves his arm in a gallant way to let me out the door first.

My free hand flaps around in the air. "I don't know. You're so nice. I mean, before Monday, I thought you were just some teasing jerk who didn't care about me at all."

"Belle," he whispers, staring into my eyes, "people aren't always what they seem."

I giggle and pretend to be that guy in the old karate movie or the kid in the cartoon *Avatar*. "Oh, wise one, you are so wise."

He grabs my gig bag off my shoulder and laughs. "Shut up and let me carry that."

"Okay," I say and watch his cute bottom strut down the corridor. I scurry after him. "Okay."

----o----

When Tom's truck parks into my driveway, the rain pours down, hammering a percussion tune against the roof and sides of my house. Down the road, just a bit, Eddie's house lights flash on and off like a warning. He left a note for me outside the house. I found it when I got home from school. A four-word note: *Sorry. I'm so sorry.* I shuddered, remembering Eddie's hand and his hard voice. What had happened to the Eddie I used to know, I have no clue.

"He's here," my mom says, rushing into my room.

I step away from my window. "I know."

My mom grabs my hands and pulls my arms away from my side. "Don't you look beautiful?"

"Mom, it's not like the prom or anything. It's just a skirt," I blush.

She pulls me into a hug. "Well, you're my beautiful baby."

Letting go, she searches my face. "You feeling strong enough to go?"

"Mom, it was just a little concussion," I say, trying to make my voice not annoyed. It doesn't work but she doesn't care, she just tweaks my nose while the doorbell rings.

She rushes off. "I better let that poor boy in from the rain."

Then she throws the kicker over her shoulder, "I was talking about your emotional health, not just your physical health, know-it-all."

Her big yellow slippers flip flop down the hallway. I turn to the mirror and put on some lip gloss. Mothers. I try not too hard to look at my face, paler than normal because of the lack of sun and too much stress. My hair will be wet soon, so there was no use struggling over that.

"Fine," I sigh at myself. "I look fine."

Tom chuckles at the door. "You sure do."

"Look who's talking?" I say, turning and smiling. He just keeps his little half grin plastered on his face while I look him up and down. His pants fit against those muscular thighs just the right way and his wet coat make his shoulders seem even broader.

He runs a hand through his brown hair. "Good show?"

I trot over to him, stand on my toes, and kiss his lips,

just a tiny, light peck that still makes me want to swoon. Then I pull away. His eyes are still closed. "You bet."

I pick up his gray, shiny tie, and it lands heavy against my palm. I finger the material. "This is?"

"Duct tape."

I let it drop against his chest, my fingers graze the wetness of his unzipped jacket.

"No quotes though?"

"Not today."

"You are one weird boy."

He shrugs and gets cocky. "That's why you like me."

"True."

He zooms into my room and comes out with Gabriel. My breath hitches inside my throat. "What are you doing?"

"We're bringing her," he says and starts hauling his butt down the hall and zips down the stairs.

"No, we're not. I'm not going to play Gabriel at the dance."

"Maybe afterwards," he says and then yells to my mom. "Good night, Mrs. Philbrick!"

"Good night, Tom!" she yells back.

But he's already gone. That boy better watch out or I'll use some duct tape on him.

----o----

The heavy rain turns to a much nicer drizzle by the time we get to school and it's dropped about ten degrees, which means it'll snow soon. Tom parks in the back lot, because the main lot is already filled. He grabs my hand and says, "Are you ready for this? Our first official-couple event?"

I raise my eyebrows. "Couple?"

"Aren't we a couple?" He leans away from me, drops my hand, and actually looks hurt.

I shrug and tease him. "I don't know. I don't remember if you ever officially asked out a pinko commie girl such as myself."

He growls and lunges at me. I scream and pretend to try to get away, but I'm not really trying. Actually, everything in my body is trying to get closer, like there's some monstrous Tom magnet that pulls my body closer. He grabs my head in his hands and his eyes flash in the light of the parking lot. "*You* are a pinko commie subversive."

"Yep," I bite my lip. "That's me."

He kisses me then, a long leaning of his body against mine, a slow rush of lips touching my own and everything in my body simultaneously sighs and sings, sighs and sings and it is such a good, good, song.

Someone pounds on the hood and Shawn jerks open Tom's door, shaking his head. He hauls Tom out and roughs up his hair. "Jesus, can't you guys even wait until after the freaking dance?"

"Nope." I hop out of my side of the car. Em smiles at me and twirls around in the drizzle.

"Nice outfit," I say, pointing at her French-looking swirly skirt and boots.

She smiles and then pouts. "It's getting wet."

"Shawn," Tom pushes him away, roughhousing him almost into the street light. "Your date is getting wet."

Shawn mutters something I can't hear. Tom gives him the finger and a smile and then follows Em and me. Because we've given up on them we are hightailing it toward the high school. She hooks her arm in mine and we bend our heads against the rain, which has now turned to part snow.

"You look happy," she says.

Shocked, I stop walking and she pulls me along. "I am."

"Good," she gives my arm a little squeeze. The sound of bass-drum beats thud out of the school. The dance is in the cafeteria, like always, real high-budget stuff. They dim the lights, move the tables, and hire this deejay guy named Mike who works at the post office in Franklin and always hits on the teachers.

I'm about to tell Em about the song in my head, which is Cliff Eberhardt singing Bob Dylan's *I Want You*, which is really funny when I think about it, because it's so obvious where my mind is. I don't get a chance to say it though because Bob comes thundering toward us from the back of the parking lot. His hair's all over the place and his white pants—yes, white pants on a boy, past Labor Day!—are wet and muddy up the side.

Em's grip on my arm gets tighter and Tom jumps up to my side and in front of me, not blocking me but ready to. I put my hand against his back.

Bob's eyes wild over and his breath sounds like he's got an asthma attack or something. "Belle . . . Belle . . ."

"What? You're talking to me now? I thought I was a freak." The words come out before I can stop them, that's how angry I am.

Tom moves from me and yanks Bob's arm so he's not looking at me. Tom's voice is total menace. "Don't even think about it, buddy."

"No. No. You don't . . . It's Dylan. Eddie Caron's about to pummel Dylan," Bob pants out.

I jerk away from Em. "Where?"

Bob points to the main parking lot, tears rush down his face. My head spins images of Dylan, dead or bleeding in some parking space somewhere.

"Bob, go in the school and get help. Em, call the police on your cell. Where's your cell?" I ask her, bulleting out instructions like some sort of army sergeant.

"It's in the car," she says. She runs back and screams, "Shawn, I need the keys to your car!"

I don't wait. I run across the parking area, the front of the school, and into the main parking lot. Tom thunders with me and then in front of me, but I keep up. Shawn catches up too.

"Don't hurt him," I murmur with every stride. "Don't hurt him."

Headlights flick by. The music in the school shifts to a slow song. The rain gets heavy again, but I don't care. I catch up to Tom and Shawn.

"We can't let him hurt him," I yell.

"We'll handle it, Belle," Shawn says and stops running. Tom and I stop, too. Because there under the streetlight is not a broken Dylan with the massive Eddie hovering over him, beating him to a pulp. Instead, Dylan pounds away at Eddie Caron, and Eddie just stands there, taking it.

Dylan, my sweet Dylan, has fists that fly like bullets, bashing against Eddie again and again. And Eddie, yeah, he's twice as big as Dylan, but he's cowering, his hands cover his head, and he yells, "Stop. Stop!"

Dylan doesn't stop. He starts kicking. His face is a twisted mask of hate. This is not my Dylan, is it? I don't know. I don't know.

I race over and grab his arm. "Dylan."

He shrugs me off and Tom and Shawn come alive then, grab him, yank him away. Eddie looks up, meets me in the eyes and his first-grade self is the one that stares, a little wounded boy looking to be a knight, searching for a princess. Blood trickles out of his nose.

"Eddie?" my voice is a whisper. He shakes his head. Rain mixes with the blood on his hands, on his nose, lightens it, sends it down to the earth. "Eddie, why didn't you fight back?"

"He said he never liked me," he shakes his head again and turns away, shoulders slumped. Then he looks back again and says in an almost whisper, "I'm so sorry what I did to you, Belle. I'm so sorry."

Then he turns away and shuffles off, one step, two. I don't understand why he hurt me. Why he let Dylan hurt him. I don't understand at all. Who is this boy? Who is Dylan? Who am I?

"Hey, Caron!" Tom yells, but I grab his tense arm. It's wet beneath my hand but I know there's warmth underneath there, warmth and strength and other good things.

"Let him go." A look passes between us. Tom understands and reaches out. His hand strokes my cheek. I nuzzle into it, and it calms me a bit, but my heart still races.

"It's stopped raining," he says, voice husky deep and full. "It's just snowing now."

I lean up on tiptoe, he leans down and then Shawn yells, "Guys."

We both turn away simultaneously to stare at Shawn. Dylan sits in a puddle in front of Shawn. Dylan's legs splay out. His hands push against his head. I look at Tom. He nods at me and I go over, reach a hand out toward Dylan's shoulder, tentatively.

"Dylan?"

His voice breaks behind his hands. "I couldn't stop, Belle."

He hiccups and gasps for breath. His hands move and wipe at his crying eyes.

"I know," I say, squatting beside him. "It's over now. He's okay."

"I couldn't stop," he repeats shaking his head, back and forth, too fast. "He hurt you."

"I'm fine, Dylan."

He keeps shaking his head. "No, you're not. He hurt you and I hurt you, Belle. *I* hurt you."

I grab his head to stop it moving. I will him to look at

me. Our eyes meet and something passes between us. It's not a golden light like that time in the bathtub, but it's something.

My voice is strong guitar chords sounding across the parking lot and into his soul. "You did *not* hurt me, Dylan. I hurt you, everybody hurt you because we wanted you to be something you aren't."

"I hurt you."

"You would have hurt me more if you kept pretending to be who I wanted you to be."

His lips tremble and he grabs at my hands. Big fluffy snowflakes stick to his wet hair, his cheeks. They melt. "I wanted to be there for you, Belle."

"I know," I say, nodding. I lift my head up to the sky. A jet plane's engines roar in the distance. It has left the Bangor Airport and zooms off to destinations unknown. I can't see its blinking red lights because of the clouds, but I know they're there. "It's okay."

The snowflakes fall down, rushing toward the earth, toward some destination they've never seen, but are just pulled toward by instinct. All of them are different, that's what science teachers tell you about snowflakes, but they really look the same.

Dylan sniffles in. "I wanted to be there."

I turn away from the white beauty dropping from the sky and stare into Dylan's eyes. "You don't need to be."

I shake my head, pull away one of my hands, glance off at Tom and his strong chest, his tree-bark good hair.

"I don't need you to be there for me, Dylan," I say. "I just need you to be there for you."

It might not make sense, but that's how it is. I give his hand a little squeeze, kiss the top of his head, and stand up. The snow already covers the parking lot. My Snoopy shoes make prints in the whiteness, tracks that lead me away from Dylan and into the arms of Tom. Like a snowflake, I'm finally pulled toward the place I'm meant to be.

WE DECIDE TO GO TO the dance anyways, because we're already here. It's pretty mellow inside. The dance-committee people have hooked up some strobe lights and a disco ball, which is so tacky that it's good. The cafeteria tables have all been cleared away and the lighting is sort of blue. The old red-haired deejay guy, Mike, is pumping out tunes that definitely do not have old white-people beats, thank God. Mr. Raines, our principal, is going around telling people, "No simulated sex acts while dancing! No humping bumps. No bumping humps!"

Basically, it's all pretty normal.

Andrew is slobbering all over this Brittney girl who is friends with Mimi. Crash is jumping up and down and crashing into people, spinning around, totally out of control and loving it.

We hang out for awhile. Shawn says he saw a cop hanging outside the gym. The cop doesn't come inside, and it wasn't Tom's dad, thank God. Em and I dance while Tom and Shawn basically stand there and slightly sway, looking embarrassed the entire time. Maine boys are NOT good dancers. I should write a list about that some time. I look around for Dylan. He's sort of hanging back, dancing with Kara and Anna and some Students for Social Justice people. Bob is there too. Bob and Dylan aren't dancing together. They're part of one big group and I feel bad for Bob for a second. I mean, they bought condoms together. They like each other. Shouldn't they be dancing together?

They're probably afraid. I make myself stop staring and focus on Em and Tom.

Then after a little while Shawn yells, "This music sucks!"

"Yep," says Tom, who winks at Shawn.

I pull on his arm. "Did you just *wink* at Shawn?"

He shakes his head and puts on this ridiculous "What? Who Me?" face.

Then he points to Andrew, who stops dry-humping Brittney long enough to bump on over to the deejay. I have a horrible feeling. It feels like when you are in an airplane and the wheels have just left the ground, but the plane lurches and it isn't smooth. Instead, it's a jarring start to what you know is going to be a rough flight.

"What is . . ." I start to say but then the deejay fades out the music super fast and speaks into the microphone.

"We've got a request for a Belle Philbrick tune and since I don't have any of those currently in the mix, I guess we're going to have to go live," he says in a super-smooth radio-guy/porn-star voice. "Belle, can you come on up here?"

I do not move. Tom and Shawn start laughing and push me forward toward the stage. Em takes a picture. Andrew's smiling and he pulls out Gabriel from behind the deejay desk. He hands her to me and then tosses Tom some keys, I guess the keys to his truck.

"Um," I say. "I really don't have anything to play."

"C'mon, Bellie Button!" Shawn yells. "Play us something."

I bite my lip and look out at all these faces, all these people I know. Kara and Anna give me a thumbs-up sign. Mimi glares. Em just keeps taking pictures like the goofy idiot she is. Tom smiles and I want to kill him. Shawn starts chanting, "Belle. Belle. Belle. Belle."

Everyone starts chanting it, everyone except Mimi, who has stalked off to the girls' room to find her broom.

"Um . . ." I say. I step up onto the little stage that's in our cafeteria for dances. It's just made out of plywood and painted black, nothing real high tech. "Um . . . You really want me to play something?"

"Yes!" Emily screams. She's jumping up and down so fast, I double check to make sure there's no trampoline under her.

Crash yells, "Rock the house down."

He makes the silly ROCK ON sign with his fingers and bangs his head back and forth, mocking himself and it makes me laugh.

"Okay," I say and get Gabriel into position and tune her a little bit, but she's not so off tonight, not as off as me. I nod. I swallow. I try to get brave. I find Tom. He smiles at me and gives me a thumbs-up sign. "Okay."

Tom points his finger down, like I'm supposed to look down, so I do. I'm good at following directions in times of stress, I guess. I mean, not that playing is stressful, but it is when you haven't played for a week. It is when you've just seen your ex-boyfriend beat someone up. And even in ordinary circumstances I have stage fright. Still, I look down.

On the floor in front of me, written in block duct-tape letters, it says, YOU CAN DO IT, BELLE.

Tom is obviously insane, but he's still lovable, ridiculously lovable.

It is silent for a minute and then I ask, "Does anybody have a tambourine?"

The freaky deejay guy has a tambourine. He pulls it out of a big, black L.L. Bean duffel bag, the kind you imagine would hide a bomb. He's also got a massive water gun in there and a box of condoms, which is just too gross to think about because he's around forty-eight years old or something. I shove my foot inside the tambourine so I can have a beat every time I press down.

Tom lets out a long, hard whistle. People start chanting my name again. Dylan is standing with Bob off to the side. They are sort of leaning on each other. Bob's holding Dylan's weight up. That's something I could never do. I'm not big enough. As much as I don't like Bob, I do like that he's there for Dylan, that he's what Dylan needs.

There are so many people here. There are my friends. There are my acquaintances who didn't know what to do about me this week, I guess. So, they stared and they whispered and tried to make sense of things. Now, they're chanting my name. Bizarre. And then there are the idiots like Mimi. I wonder if they'll heckle me. I wonder if I'll care.

"Play for us, Bellie!" Shawn yells.

"Do it, Belle!" Dylan's melody voice hollers out. He's

smiling at me. Somehow despite everything that just happened, he's smiling.

If Dylan can smile. I can play. It's time. I can tell you one thing. I'm not playing a show tune. I'm not playing any Barbra Streisand. It's going to be something hard and good and alive.

"Okay. Okay, I'll play one," I say to the smile, to the cafeteria, to everyone.

In the dark dance-light of the cafeteria, my body straightens up on the stage, reaching, and my soul, it floats up by the ceiling, watching it all, wondering about this crazy girl with one foot ready to stomp out time on a tambourine, this girl ready to sing some part of herself to everybody, this girl who is me.

My mind is like the river outside Crash's house, just this vast flowing thing that moves and sways with the music that flies out of Gabriel, but there's no thoughts going on, no big secrets. It's just me, my fingers, and music, and eventually words flow out of my mouth, like offerings to the river, floating under those gloomy Maine skies, trying to break up the gray with little bursts of light. Seconds pass. Moment pass.

I play and I play and my fingers remember all the positions, all the notes. My shoulder stretches above the weight of my guitar, but it's good, it's so good that for a little bit even my headache goes away. I strum and strum and stomp and sing until the song finally ends.

About the Author

Carrie Jones likes Skinny Cow fudgicles and potatoes. She does not know how to spell fudgicles. This has not prevented her from writing books. She lives with her cute family in Maine. She has a large, skinny white dog and a fat cat. Both like fudgicles. Only the cat likes potatoes. This may be a reason for the kitty's weight problem (Shh . . . don't tell). Carrie has always liked cowboy hats but has never owned one. This is a very wrong thing. She graduated from Vermont College's MFA program for writing. She has edited newspapers and poetry journals and has won awards from the Maine Press Association and also been awarded the Martin Dibner Fellowship as well as a Maine Literary Award. She is still not sure why.

Tips on Writing Acknowledgements:

1. Make sure you thank people who are related to you and put up with you saying things like: I stink. Man, do I stink. What am I doing this for?

   a. Thanks to Em and Doug, for always having faith in me when I couldn't even figure out what the word "faith" meant. Your love means everything.

2. Make sure you thank the people who fed you for eighteen years, have seen your bottom naked, and lived to tell the tale. A-hem.

   a. Thanks to my parents, Betty Morse and Llewellyn Barnard, for being goofy, AND loving, AND supportive.

3. Make sure you thank people you tormented your entire life, who put up with their younger sister and her poor taste in shoes and her lack of organizational skills and inability to send birthday cards on time. I buy them. I just forget to mail them. I swear.

   a. Thanks to my sister, Deb, and my brother, Bruce.

4. Make sure you thank your grandmothers, because they saw your naked bottom, too, and they could theoretically sell photos. BUT THEY WON'T!

   a. Thanks to my Nana, Rena Morse, and my Grammy, Florence Barnard, for your love of words.

5. Thank the mentors who made you write better because they put up with you saying things like "I'm sorry this is stinks so bad." There's no amount of money that can pay for that.

   a. Thanks to Kathi Appelt, Sharon Darrow, Tim Wynne-Jones, and Rita Williams-Garcia for your brilliance and encouragement.

6. You HAVE TO THANK your editors! This is terribly important. Now, what are their names again? Just kidding.

   a. Thanks, Andrew Karre, for being the best editor I could ever ask for and for all your beautiful patience during my telephone tangents. You made this book a thousand times better than when it first crossed your desk. Thanks for snatching it up.

   b. Thanks, Rhiannon Ross, for believing in this book and for making me believe in it again. Your emails made my year.

7. You also HAVE TO THANK your agent, but even if I didn't have to, I would because he is STELLAR and BRILLIANT and AMAZING.

   a. Thank you, Edward Necarsulmer IV, a great knight, a kind soul, and a snazzy dresser even if you've never worn a flannel shirt . . . okay, maybe because of that.

8. Make sure you thank your friends who put up with you whining and not always answering the phone.

   a. Thanks to the Whirligigs at Vermont College. The best class of writers ever. There is nothing wrong with being freakishly close.

   b. Thanks to Grady Holloway, Don Radovich, Jennifer Osborn, and Dottie Vachon for eating lunch with me.

c. Thanks to Chris Maselli, Emily Wing Smith, Johanna Staley, and Bruce Frost, for making me feel safe and loved, even when I was far from home.

9. Breathe. This list is so long. Worry if other authors' lists are so long. Decide not to care. Make sure you thank two of your favorite people of all time.
   a. Thanks to Emily Ciciotte and Belle Vachon for loaning my book your first names.

10. Thank important people that you love.
   a. Thanks to Joe Tullgren, my first gay boyfriend, and most likely not my only gay boyfriend. You are the best and you taught me so much about love.

11. Thank the guy who taught you more about writing than anyone else in the entire world, the guy who made you believe in yourself, the best high school writing teacher the world has ever known.
   a. Thank you Joseph Sullivan. Someday, Mr. Sullivan, one of us is going to get you that damn beach house. I swear it.

12. Stop thanking people now. Whew. Go ask Nice Editor Man if list is too long.

13. Ignore what he says if it's negative. Tell him he's a super editor guy if it's positive. Yay!